That "D" On the Side

(Women Cheat Too)

Nika Michelle

Author's Dedication/Note

A special thank you to all of my faithful readers and those of you who are reading something by me for the first time. I am truly blessed to be able to do what I do and I thank you all for making it worth it.

Thank you to the Lord for giving me the gift of writing. I couldn't think of anything that I'd rather do.

Thank you to my parents and my siblings as well as my huge and supportive family as a whole. Not to mention a special shout out to all of those who support me.

Blessings and I hope you all enjoy…

There is a storm cuming,

but not from the skies.

This storm that is brewing

is right between your thighs.

I can hear the thunder roaring

and feel the lightening coursing

passionately through my veins.

As my blood flows, I grow

in anticipation of navigating

the flood from your rain.

Chapter 1

Fanci

"I can't believe that I agreed to do this shit," I hissed with an attitude as I stared at the sign that read "Tats & All Dat". Really? How ghetto could a person be to name their tattoo shop that? Then I had to take into consideration that I was in my old neighborhood.

"Uhh, you didn't agree to it heifer. You lost a bet and so, you have no choice. Now get your scared ass up out of this car and let's do this," my best friend Janai said with a mischievous grin on her cute, cocoa brown face.

She was right. We'd been doing the "bet thing" since we were little and I always seemed to be the one who lost. Janai constantly had me doing something crazy. When she lost, which was rare, my demands were never as outlandish as hers. That was probably because I had become accustomed to a different lifestyle and so my thoughts were different too. Although she was successful also, it was somewhat hard to get that hood side out of her.

We both grew up in a low income area on the South Side of Decatur, but we had both risen above our past circumstances. Janai was a Certified

Personal Accountant and I was one of her clients because I owned my own business. We'll get into all of that a little later.

"Is it too late for me to decline? You know I always said I'd never get a tattoo. Unlike you, the thought of mutilating my body is not appealing and what kind of name is Tats and all Dat any damn way?"

Janai glared at me as she shook her head. "It's called that because they not only do tattoos, but they also do piercings and they sell clothes and sneakers."

"Oh wow, like I said ghetto as hell. You can get a tat, pierce your nipple and buy some J's. A hood ass one stop shop." I shook my head. "I still can't believe I let you talk me into this shit."

"Girl, you done forgot where you came from for real. Do you not remember growing up less than three blocks from here?" Janai shook her head and got out of the car. "C'mon woman. You might as well just get it over with, because if you don't the alternative will be much worse."

"Oh, I remember very well," I huffed as I climbed out of the car. "You won't let me forget and what the hell is the alternative? It couldn't possibly be worse than this."

Janai rolled her eyes as she slammed the door of her black Range Rover. "You are a trip woman."

I managed to let out a sarcastic laugh. "So I'm wrong for wanting a different life than what we were handed as children?"

"No, shit, I want that too. I'm just saying you don't have to turn your nose up when you come back here like you're better than everybody else. You were fortunate enough to get out of here, but that doesn't mean that your shit doesn't smell just as bad as the folks who are still stuck right where you don't want to be." She opened the door of the tattoo shop and stood there so that I could walk inside first.

I sighed. "Alright damn. You made your point. Now let me get the smallest tattoo on the most discrete place on my body, so I can get on with my busy day."

That time when Janai rolled her eyes at me she laughed hard as hell. "What busy day? You ain't got shit to do but work the hell out of my nerves."

Ok, so you may be wondering why we are best friends since we seem to gripe at each other so much. We usually got along just fine, but when it came to our old hood, we never seemed to see eye to eye. I was glad to get out of there and rarely went back. Janai on the other hand, frequently visited her family and friends who were still there, and patronized the businesses.

"I have plenty of shit to do thank you very much."

"Orgasma literally runs itself. All you have to do is click some keys to ship out fake dicks, vibrating bullets and sex swings. You do that by swiping away at your laptop's keys. You don't even have to do anything because all of the merchandise is shipped from the warehouse and your employees do all of the hard work," she reminded me as if I didn't know what my business entailed.

Orgasma was my business that I mentioned earlier. It was obvious that I owned a very lucrative, virtual sex toy utopia, well…store. Anything you could think of to pleasure yourself, someone else, or more than one, was available on my website.

"Oh, there's way more to it than that and you know it," I spat with narrowed eyes.

"Whatever. Come on boo. Just stop fighting it. You are getting this tattoo, so it's really no point in us going back and forth about it."

She grabbed my arm and pulled me toward the large, black framed posters along the wall that displayed thousands of tattoo options. About five minutes into the search for the perfect tat and I was a little bit more into it. Maybe some sexy body art wouldn't be so bad. Janai had two small tattoos and they were well hidden because she was a professional woman.

My business was a little taboo, but I made a lot of money selling sex toys online. It was easy to market something that most people used on a daily basis and in this day and age everybody was experimenting in the bedroom. The porn industry kept me in business because sex toys were used a lot during filming. When they ordered they bought everything in bulk because it was not sanitary to share sex toys. I also had plenty of private sellers all over the US who often had "sex toy parties" to get the merchandise to the consumers upfront. The money was pouring in and I was loving it.

"So, you decided yet?" Janai asked. Suddenly her voice was all calm and sweet.

I glanced over at her and shook my head. "No, not really."

She sighed and threw her long, bouncy, honey blonde weave over her shoulder as she glared at me with her icy gray contacts. "Why don't you stop acting like that? You just said you wanted to get a strawberry on your..."

"Want to? I have no choice right?" I didn't wait for her response as I continued.

"This is not a want, but a need. I need to hurry up and get a damn tattoo so we can leave. If I had known that stupid ass bet..."

"See anything you like?" A deep voice interrupted my rant.

I turned around in annoyance, but damn, he was extra fine with a side of sexy. I definitely saw something that I liked. Suddenly my frown turned upside down. I was married, but it was okay for me to have a little innocent fun.

"Do you work here?" Janai asked with her eyes on me and my sly grin.

"Yeah, I'm Devin. I own the place." His smile was dazzling. "Can I help you ladies?"

Oh, he was just too damn proud of his little hood spot. How cute.

I spoke up. "Well Devin, I'm personally not into tattoos, but I lost a bet and getting inked was the terms." My smile was flirtatious, but I controlled myself against my will.

Not only did he have nice, thick lips, but his teeth were also white and straight. He had a Denzel Washington type of smile. I also noticed a faint scar right above his cheek. It was kind of sexy. Otherwise his skin was like smooth, milk chocolate and he had dark, wavy hair that was cut close to my liking. His beard and moustache were neatly trimmed. He looked well kept, but his hard exterior made it obvious that he had a past in the streets. From the way he carried himself I wondered if he still dabbled in hood activities, although he had his own business.

"Well, do you know what you want to get?" His voice was deep and rich. I also noticed that he had a northern accent.

If only he knew what I really wanted to get. My eyes were glued to his broad chest and bulging biceps. At about 6'3, he had the body of a star NFL player. Dayum! Mmm mmm mmm. I was really hoping that he would be the one to do my tattoo.

"I think I want to keep it simple, since I've never done this before." I bit my bottom lip and batted my lash extensions at him. "I kind of want to get a strawberry like on my foot or something. Uh, will you be doing it for me?"

"I can definitely do it for you...uh, what's your name beautiful?"

I bet he could. His eyes were all over my curvaceous frame and I couldn't help but blush. Janai cleared her throat loudly.

"I'm Fanci," I said quickly as I reached out to shake his hand.

"Oh, so you fancy huh?" He let out a laugh referring to the song by Drake, Swizz Beats and TI. "That's your real name?" His eyebrow rose in curiosity.

I let out a cute little giggle. "Yes, my mother really named me Fanci."

His eyes drifted to Janai. "You getting inked too…?"

"Janai." She shook his extended hand. "And no. I'm just here with her."

"Are you two gorgeous ladies sisters?" He asked with that smile still plastered on his handsome face.

It only added to his handsomeness. The way he was standing there looking all perfectly manly in jeans that fit just right and a gray True Religion tee shirt was doing something to me. It was mid May, so the weather was nice.

"No, we're best friends, but you can say that we're like sisters though."

He nodded and then his smile faded. "You said that you want the tat on your foot right?"

"Yes."

"Where on your foot? I'm going to be honest with you. The foot is a bony part of the body and is probably the most painful. You should get it on a muscular part of your body like the upper arm, or the calf. I mean, either way you're gonna feel some pain. It's just all about what you can and can't take." As he talked he stared deeply into my eyes and occasionally licked his lips.

I felt my whole body start to overheat instantly.

Janai cleared her throat again and lightly nudged me with her elbow. I was in a trance, so it was good that she'd kind of snapped me out of it.

"Okay, well, I guess I'll get it on my calf then. As long as it's small that'll be fine." I really didn't want my husband to notice it, but I knew that he would.

Janai shook her head as a huge smile spread across her face.

"Cool." His eyes drifted over toward the receptionist desk. "Go fill out the necessary paper work and I'll be ready for you in a few minutes. Okay?" That sexy ass smile was back.

I nodded. "Okay."

He walked off and I just stood there and stared at his wide back, slender waist, and nice butt. I couldn't help but shake my head. I could only imagine how muscular and defined his body was.

"That is one sexy ass man," I said under my breath.

"Hell yeah," Janai agreed breathlessly. "And he's bow-legged too. Mmm."

"I can only imagine…"

"Tell me about it and he wants you."

"Girl bye. I'm a married woman."

"True, but a little flirting ain't never hurt nobody."

I laughed and turned to go to the receptionist desk. "Your ass is gonna get me in trouble in here."

Her laughter rang out behind me.

* * *

Less than an hour later I was admiring my new tattoo in the full length mirror.

"It looks really good," Janai complimented my body art, which made me feel better about it.

One thing I didn't need was validation from people, but my bestie's opinion always mattered.

"You like it?" Devin asked with a look of curiosity on his face.

"Actually I love it." I had let him and Janai talk me into adding my name under the strawberry.

It was written in fancy incursive letters, which suited my name just fine. My mother, the feisty Clarine Taylor, told me that she had given me that name so that I could live up to it. Although my neighborhood and surroundings were the opposite of my namesake, she always made sure that I had everything that I wanted as well as needed. Most people said that she lived above her means, but in my eyes she just wanted the best for me. I would always love my mother for that.

"Good. Here's the print out with instructions on how to care for your tattoo. Be sure to keep it clean and use A&D Ointment to help it heal. Now I'm going to cover it with a bandage, but I want you to remove it and clean it within the next hour." He looked at me with concern like I was his patient. Hmm, he could be my doctor any day.

"Yes sir. That shit hurt like hell, but I'm kind of glad I did it." I smiled as he gently pressed the tape against my skin to hold the bandage that looked like what a butcher would put under the meat in a grocery store.

Janai looked taken aback. "Are you really? I had to literally pull you out of the car kicking and screaming to get your ass in here."

I put my finger to my lips to get her to shut the hell up. "Okay, so I was a little nervous at first, but..."

"A little..."

"Uh, thank you so much Devin." I cut her off just as he stood up.

"I'm sorry that I hurt you. I tried my best to be gentle," he said sincerely.

I stared into his sexy, cognac colored eyes with the long lashes and sighed. If only I was single.

"Yeah, I know, but the needle obviously didn't care about how gentle you were trying to be." I laughed and then my cell phone rang inside of my purse. "Excuse me."

I fished it out and saw Isaac flash across the screen. The hubby was calling to inquire about my whereabouts I was sure. Without a second thought I sent him straight to the voicemail.

"You ready to go boo?" Janai asked.

I guess I wasn't trying to budge. Shit, I thought about getting another tattoo just so he'd have a reason to touch me again. Although it had been painful, I liked the fact that a man who looked like him had his hands on me. It was a little bit crazy how strongly I was attracted to him, but I had to ignore it.

"Yes," I breathed. "Is there anything else I need to know Devin?"

Shit, I wanted to know his phone number and his address too, but I kept that to myself.

"No, you're good."

"Do I pay you?"

"No, you can pay up front on the side of the shop where the clothes are. Your total will be one hundred even," he said as she removed his gloves and threw them in the trash.

"Okay, well, thank you again." I reached out to shake his hand as an excuse to touch him one last time.

"My pleasure."

That damn smile.

I shook my head and followed Janai so that I could pay for my service.

"So, getting a tat wasn't so bad thanks to that sexy ass hunk of chocolate huh?" Janai asked knowingly.

"He made it worth it. That's for damn sure."

We both laughed.

*　　*　　*

An hour later I was back at my beautiful 5,000 square foot mini mansion in a gated community in Alpharetta. Of course I would aspire to live a privileged lifestyle in one of Georgia's most affluent suburbs, because my mother had drilled that into my head at an early age. She had always wanted me to do better than her and so in order to make her proud I made sure that I did. Now she was benefiting from it all because I made sure that she did not have to live in that awful neighborhood she had raised me in.

Although Janai had just dropped me off, we were on the phone time I closed my front door.

"Is Isaac there?" She asked knowing that he wouldn't approve of my tattoo.

That was nonsense being that I was an independent woman who owned a sex toy business. He hadn't seen the tattoo yet though and I hadn't told him about it.

"Yeah, he's in his study getting drunk as usual while he pretends to do some imaginary work. I swear, I care for my husband, but a miserable marriage is not what I envisioned for myself."

"Well, that takes us back to our bet. Angie was miserable with Don, so she did what she had to do. I keep telling you…"

I cut her off real quick. "I'm not divorcing Isaac. We'll get through it. We always do."

She sighed. "Okay, but you lost the bet because you thought Angie was going to work it out with him, but I knew that she was serious about filing for a divorce."

Angie was Janai's personal assistant. She was a Puerto Rican beauty who was married to her high school sweet heart. Don owned a very successful detail shop called Whipped that could turn anybody's car into a dream ride. He was famous nationally for equipping luxury rides with rims, tinted windows and all types of unnecessary crap that people liked to add to their cars. He was always featured in car magazines and entering contests for his creations. On the outside looking in people would've thought he was the idea catch, but he wasn't. He made Angie's life a living hell by being a controlling, condescending asshole.

So, Janai and I had a bet. I didn't think Angie had the nerve to leave him, because of the lifestyle that he provided for her, and Janai did not agree with me. She just knew that Angie would really file for divorce like she'd been threatening to do for years. Come to find out she did and the divorce had been finalized a couple days before my best friend dragged me to that tattoo shop.

"Well, that's Angie and Donnie's situation. I'm in a totally different situation with Isaac. I mean, he is an older man and he drinks a lot, so I'm suffering from lack of dick and affection over here, but other than that…" My voice trailed off and I let out a stiff laugh.

"You're only twenty eight and you're married to a man who is almost fifty. Of course his sex drive is going to be lower than yours. You don't deserve to be in a marriage that you're not being satisfied in. You have your own business and you can stand on your own two feet. I know bitch. I handle your finances."

I let out a deep breath as I undressed. "I know, but if it wasn't for him I wouldn't have any of that."

"Okay, that's fine and dandy, but he's not satisfying you Fanc! You have to think about yourself. You're still young. Don't you want children? It's really fucked up that he snuck and got a vasectomy behind your back. Not only that, but his mom's a real bitch. Why deal with that woman if you don't have to. You're in a loveless marriage and that's not healthy. You're his trophy wife and I don't think he treats you right."

My best friend had a point, but shit was a whole lot more complicated than she'd ever know. At least he didn't put his hands on me. I stared at myself in the mirror knowing that I was an attractive woman. I wasn't the most beautiful woman in the world, but I wasn't the worst looking either. I was 5'6, and weighed a thick 155 pounds. My curves were my confidence and I loved the way God had made me. My breasts were perfect, round C cups, my waist line wasn't the slimmest, but I knew how to suck it in and my hips and ass were like POW! My thighs and calves were thick and I was blessed with nice facial features to pull it all together.

My skin was the color of coffee with a touch of cream. The voluptuous, pouty lips that I was blessed with came from my beloved mother. I never really knew my father, but wondered if my round nose and mysterious, light brown slanted eyes had come from him. My shoulder length thick, coarse hair was always done to perfection. I could afford to keep my nails and toes done as well as my wardrobe adorned with designer labels. Still, I wasn't happy with all that I'd been blessed with.

"Isaac's a good man, but he's under a lot of pressure right now." I was always making excuses for him, but a marriage was for better or for worse right?

"You didn't even love him at first. I thought it was all about the convenience and you would divorce him after you got your…"

I heard footsteps on the other side of the bedroom door. "I have to go Nai. I'll call you later."

"Okay, but think about what I said."

"I will."

The door swung open just as I pressed the end button.

"What are you doing?" Isaac's speech was slurred as if he'd been drinking all day.

He was the Dean of students at an HBCU in the area, but he was a biology professor at Clark when I met him ten years ago. At the time I was a freshman. We'd been married for seven years. It was the weekend, so he was wasted of course.

"I'm about to take a shower baby. Is that a problem?" I asked sarcastically as I removed my earrings and placed them in one of my jewelry boxes.

He walked over to me reeking of alcohol and that nasty pipe that he always smoked. That old man shit was getting on my nerves. Suddenly an image of Devin flashed into my mind. Damn, I really missed dealing with men my age. Maybe all of the money in the world wasn't worth what I was being subjected to.

Isaac was still a handsome man and when I first met him I was physically attracted to him. Back then the relationship was exciting and he romanced me until I was dizzy. After he won me over, I dropped out of college my junior year and became his wife. His money was my agenda though, because the sex had never been that great. In my opinion sex came second to my coins and I wanted those coins more than anything else.

Now at the age of 49 Isaac's age was starting to show. His caramel colored skin didn't look as youthful. The crow's feet around his eyes and the wrinkles on his forehead were getting deeper. His salt and pepper hair was getting grayer and his once solid physique was starting to turn into mush. I hated the way his belly protruded and he was starting to get man titties. At one point I could stand looking at him naked, but lately he repulsed me.

"Can I get in with you?" He asked as he pulled me into his arms.

I tried not to show that I was turned off by his drunken demeanor. Maybe a shower was best for him. As I stared into his hazel eyes I felt like I didn't know how much more I could take. If only things could be more simple.

"Sure," I said as I let out a sharp breath.

At least it would wash away the horrid smell and maybe sober him up a little.

His hands were groping me and I was still thinking about Devin. As he kissed me sloppily I wondered if Devin's kisses were more precise. They probably were. I longed for passion and for the ravenous love making that I'd been craving. As my husband stepped in the shower with me, I thought about another man. A man that I didn't even know.

Chapter 2

Devin

"Damn woman! Why the hell you knockin' on my door like the police!" I was staring into the menacing, dark brown eyes of my three year old daughter's mother Amil.

"Y'en answer yo' phone so I came over. Yo' child wanted to see you!" She actually maintained eye contact with me as she sold me that bullshit.

It was after ten pm and she was holding our sleeping child in her arms. There was no way that she was there because Londyn wanted to see me. Besides, she was the parent and it was late. Even if my child did want to see me, she should've just called to let me speak to her instead of bringing her out. My problem with Amil had always been the fact that her hood rat tendencies made her make the worst decisions.

"Stop playin' yourself Mil. You know damn well you just wanted to see if I had a woman over here." I shook my head at her desperation.

She was a pretty, thick lil' something, but her lack of morals drove me crazy. Her folks had never really been there for her, so that pulled at my heart strings, but maybe that made her parenting skills lacking. I didn't have the best parents in the world either, but I wanted to be a better father than mine. That was why I was hell bent on turning my life around.

"So, you got a bitch over here or what? Let me in nigga? Our child is sleep and I wanna lay her down." Her eyes were pleading with me and for some reason I'd been weak for that woman since I moved to Atlanta from Washington, DC at the age of sixteen.

Her parenting skills had been what broke us up two years ago and my goal was to get full custody of my daughter. The only thing about that was the fact that I had a criminal record. Getting my daughter wasn't going to be as easy as I wanted it to be, but I wasn't going to give up the fight. Once my daughter was born I left my past behind and invested the dirty money I'd managed to stash in my businesses. Not only did I have the tattoo shop, but I also owned a car wash. A year before Londyn was born I had just been released from prison for armed robbery. My little girl had been my saving grace.

If it wasn't for her I'd probably still be robbing dope boys and laying up with her trifling ass mama.

"Gone and lay her down in her bed and then you can leave. I'm off tomorrow…so…"

That wasn't what she wanted to hear. "Why the fuck you gotta act like that Devin?" There were tears in her eyes. "I been in love wit' you since I was fifteen and you gon' treat me like I'm just some stranger! Really? I'm the mother of yo'…"

I cut her off. "Keep your voice down woman. I know that you're the mother of my child. Don't keep holdin' that shit over my head. I take care of mine and you know that."

As I shook my head she glared at me with anger in her eyes. "If you ain't gon' be wit' me I'll make sure you don't see your daughter either. I'll go to court and tell them to take away yo' rights 'cause of your violent criminal record. We a package deal nigga, so if you don't want me, you don't want her. Shit, why you think I had her, huh? I ain't want no damn kids. I had a baby for you, 'cause you wanted one and you gon' leave me to fend for myself. You selfish son of a bitch. I tell ya what. You won't be happy nigga and no bitch will ever be happy wit' you. I'll make sure of that. Misery loves company and as long as I'm miserable yo' ass gon' be right there wit' me. You can bet that shit." The look on her face let me know that she meant every word of what she'd said.

I was so tempted to grab my child from her arms, and lock the damn door, but I knew that she'd run to the cops and say that I kidnapped her. Shit, I was on parole and I only had five more months to go. A nigga did not have time for that bullshit. I had to make sure that I kept my cool and went about things the right way. I couldn't risk my chances of getting my daughter, so I didn't lose it.

"Whatever. You can threaten me all you want, but I ain't gon' fall in your trap. Take yo' ass home. I'll come get my daughter in the mornin'." With that said I slammed the door in her face and walked off to go to my room.

I owned a nice, two bedroom condo in Lithonia, GA not far from the Stonecrest Mall area. Something told me that my ratchet ass baby mama wouldn't cause a scene, or maybe that was wishful thinking. I was hoping she'd just leave in the black Benz that I had bought for her.

I didn't mind owning businesses in the hood, but after I became a father I didn't want to live there anymore. I wanted my daughter to be in a safe place, so she had her own bedroom at my crib and everything. I even made sure that her mom was straight with a nice apartment in the East Lake Village subdivision in Atlanta. There was a really good charter school over there that I wanted her to attend the following year.

Before I could lay on my bed and chill in front of my big screen TV the doorbell started ringing and then the loud knocking started again. I stumped toward the front door in anger. I couldn't believe Amil. Why did she seem to starve for drama and attention? I paid child support, gave her money and I spent time with Londyn. What more did she want?

I opened the door with a look of contempt on my face.

"What the hell is wrong wit' you…"

"Daddy…"

When I looked down and noticed that my daughter was awake, I lowered my voice.

"Can we come in please? Your child wanted to see you like I said." Amil's tone was taunting.

I knew that she woke Londyn up on purpose and I didn't want to make a scene in front of her.

"C'mon," I said with a sigh as I stepped aside.

Amil stepped inside and I closed the door behind her. I reached for my daughter feeling good about the fact that at least I knew where she was. Her mama was known for leaving her with just about anybody to go out to the club or to do who knew what else. As I held her in my arms I thought about what I had to do to get full custody. My chances were slim, but I had to do whatever I had to do. I couldn't give up on the process like most men did out of fear of the system, or pure lack of patience.

"You still sleepy baby girl?" I asked as she yawned and then rested her head on my shoulder.

"Yes daddy. Can I sleep with you?" She rubbed her eyes and then closed them.

I glanced over at Amil. "You're the only lady daddy wants in his bed tonight. Give me her bag Mil. You can leave now."

"What did I tell you? Package deal nigga." She took Londyn's overnight bag off her shoulder and placed it on the sofa.

"Umm, you must be crazy. You ain't spendin' the night. You claimed she wanted me and now she got me. Why the hell you still here? Go to the apartment that I pay for in the car that I pay for." I shook my head, grabbed Londyn's bag and went to my bedroom to lay her down.

When I didn't hear the front door close I knew that I was going to have a time getting that woman out of my crib. She was not giving up and that shit was really starting to get to me. I wanted to blow up, but I tried to keep the peace for my daughter's sake. She was all that I had and I had to pacify her mom at times so that I'd have the upper hand. Still, I wasn't one to give her mixed messages. I didn't want to be with her, so I cut out the physical part of our relationship almost a year ago.

When I walked back in the room Amil was standing there butt ass naked. Her long, bone straight weave hung down to her lower back, giving her a sexy, exotic look. Her mocha colored skin was flawless and her almond shaped eyes sparkled with mischief as she flashed those dimples at me. There was a look of intent on her face, and although her body was enticing me, I couldn't go there with her.

"Put your clothes back on yo'." I grabbed them off the floor and passed them to her. "What if our daughter walks in here?"

She rolled her eyes. "She done seen me naked before."

"Hmm, I wonder what else she's seen."

She grabbed her clothes. "What the fuck is that supposed to mean."

"You know what it means. You ain't a nominee for the mama of the year award woman. I mean look at you. Got your daughter out late at night worryin' 'bout what the fuck I'm doin'. Then when I tell you to leave yo' desperate ass wake her up knowin' that's yo' way of gettin' yo' ass in here. Now here yo' ass is standin' butt naked in my livin' room tryna seduce a nigga." I shook my head. "You ain't got no shame at all. None. What the hell?" I had no idea what I ever saw in her.

"Fuck you! I can't believe you think a woman who looks like me is desperate. Nigga, I can have any mufuckin' man I want, but I chose yo' sorry ass!" She put her shirt on with an attitude.

"Sorry?" I let out a sarcastic chuckle. "Yeah right. What other nigga would make sure you got a roof over yo' head and a car to drive without fuckin' yo' ass. I don't want yo' pussy ma. I just want you to be a good mother to our child. That's all the fuck I want from you."

"Well I want my family back nigga! That's what the fuck I want! What about what the fuck I want!" She screamed as she pulled her jeans on.

"Calm yo' ass down," I said in a hushed tone. "That's why you ain't got yo' family. You don't know how to act like a fuckin' adult. I'm not gon' be wit' a grown woman who acts like a big ass kid. Our daughter acts older than you."

She rolled her eyes and threw her hands up. "Wow. Really?" Her hand was on her hip. "You never cease to amaze me Devin. I act like a big kid? You're the big ass kid. You're the one who acts like every fuckin' thing has to go your way or no way. You're the fuckin' childish one. If it wasn't for me your ass would've got twenty fuckin' years in prison, but I lied for yo' ass. They never found shit in your crib because of me. You owe me! You just got one charge instead of the rack of charges you were facin' at first. That was 'cause of me. Remember that shit. Not only that, but I held you down for the three years you were in there!"

"Don't keep throwin' that in my face. I do more for you than I have to and you know it. And speakin' of somebody havin' to have their way ain't you the one who said if I'm not wit' you I can't see my child? That sounds really damn selfish and childish if you ask me."

"Well I ain't ask you!" She snapped and grabbed her purse. "I'm gonna leave, but I meant every word I said about makin' your life and the life of any woman that you try to be wit' a livin' fuckin' hell. I know it sounds cliché, but if I can't have you no bitch will. You belong to me. I don't have your name tattooed on me for nothing. You branded me as yours and you're stuck wit' me nigga. Know that and marinate on that shit. You rejected me tonight, but you won't keep doin' that shit when you look around and see that I'm the only bitch willin' to deal wit' your ass!" She turned in her six inch stiletto heels and walked toward the door.

I wanted to grab her and throw her out on her ass, but I just stood there in amazement as she walked out and slammed the door. That woman had the audacity to try to force me to be with her. When I did decide to be with somebody I would have to make sure that I already had custody of my daughter. For the time being Londyn was my top priority. I mean, I was a twenty nine year old man who loved beautiful women, but I wasn't rushing anything.

Speaking of women that damn Fanci was sexy as hell and she seemed to be so refined. She was the exact opposite of Amil. Damn, I couldn't get her curvy frame and natural beauty out of my mind. She seemed like she would be the perfect mother for Londyn, but at that point in my life I wasn't interested in a serious relationship. My focus was on my money and my kid. Besides, she hadn't shown any interest in me anyway. Yeah, she was a little flirtatious, but it hadn't gone any further than that.

I had started to ask for her number, but after a few bad experiences with women that I met at the shop, I decided to keep it professional. At that point I could kick myself for that shit, because before Amil came over that damn Fanci was on my mind. Something told me that I would see her again. There was just some kind of chemistry between us and I knew that she had to feel it too.

"Daddy, I want some juice," I heard Londyn say behind me.

I quickly pushed Fanci out of my mind, but it would only be temporary. At that point she was etched in my mental and there was no way I could run away from that. Damn, I was all fucked up over a woman that I didn't even know.

* * *

"Sup Trav?" I greeted my business partner and best friend since high school.

Travis was about 5'11, with pecan brown skin and shoulder length dreadlocks. He was slim, but not bony. One thing about him was he was an honest, hardworking person that I could trust.

He had invested in the car wash with me, but unlike me, he'd taken the straight and narrow path before being slapped with prison time. When I was locked up he was working as a manager at a furniture store. Because of his management experience he managed the car wash. Our home girl Gina managed the tattoo shop. In our younger days we all ran the streets together, but Travis's mother stayed on his ass. For that reason he gave it all up before I did. I didn't have my mother around then. I was getting into so much trouble in Washington, DC that she sent me to live with my father in Decatur.

The crazy thing about that was my father didn't even discipline me as much as she did. He was so busy chasing skirts that he didn't have time for me. Therefore I ended up in the streets even harder. I loved fast money and so instead of selling drugs, I got a crew together with Travis and we robbed the drug dealers. Sometimes we would involve Gina, who would set up dope boys from out of town. We got so much money doing that shit that it was ridiculous. Of course that shit caught up with us eventually, so me and my boy gave up the street life for very different reasons.

When our boy Andre was murdered during a robbery gone wrong, Travis was out for good. Not me though. I was addicted to the money and the adrenaline rush. Holding a gun to a nigga's head and taking his shit was the rush that I needed back then. Now all I needed was the rush of my daughter's love because I was lucky to still be alive.

I ended up catching a case of course and it was really wild the way it happened. Out of the blue, my nigga Brian decided that we should rob a well-known drug dealer in the hood named Ray. That shit had to be divine intervention because as we were leaving the scene the cops were coming in to do a bust. What were the fucking chances of that shit happening? Of course we ended up getting arrested too because they had the spot wrapped up. Honestly, that situation had probably saved my life.

"Ain't shit man. Just dropped my lil' princess off wit' her triflin' ass mama." The thought of Amil made my blood boil.

"Don't let her get to you. You need some new pussy man. You act like you don't even like women no more. Let me find out you…"

"Shut the fuck up before I shoot you Trav. I don't play that shit man. You know I'm focused on business and raisin' my daughter."

Travis laughed as he took a bite of his Subway sandwich. I had decided to stop at the car wash to check up on shit before I headed back to the crib to chill with a cold one and some ESPN. Usually that was what my Sundays entailed.

"Calm down killer. I'm just sayin'. Amil ain't never been all there man. You let a big butt and a smile get you. It's okay though. Don't beat yourself up. Most of us niggas fall victim to that shit, but you gotta learn from it man. At least you got a beautiful daughter out of the deal. I'm just glad I left Amil's girl Porscha alone when I did." He shook his head. "Birds of a fuckin' feather. I'm just happy to be married to a good woman who takes good care of our children."

His wife Deidre *was* a good catch. He had met her about seven years ago and they had two children. Their son was four and their daughter had just turned two. Deidre was a hairstylist who had her own salon in their basement, so she wasn't on that gold digging shit like Amil. Trav had always warned me about her, but I thought I was in love. True, I'd had chicks on the side during our relationship, but they couldn't take me away from my lady. Hmm, after a while I saw Amil for who she truly was.

She claimed that she held me down when I was in the pen, but I had heard differently. After she got pregnant with Londyn I started getting wind of the rumors. At first I didn't believe them, but the truth ended up coming out. Trav didn't want to tell me at first, but he had seen her out with numerous dudes. Because of that I got a DNA test after Londyn was born. I had to make sure that she was mine before I dedicated myself to fatherhood.

Like a fool I forgave Amil after it was proven that Londyn was mine. In my mind she was human and needed some type of companionship when I was gone. She wasn't equipped to be a committed woman though and I wasn't going to be played. I was the man in the relationship not her. Shit, it wasn't justified, but men were the ones who usually cheated. We never wanted to see our women in that light. If I could attempt to be faithful she could too. After I caught her out and about with some nigga and my daughter was with them, that was the last straw. I was officially done trying to work it out with her ass. All I wanted to do was take care of my seed.

"So, other than baby mama drama what's goin' on in your world?" His mouth was full as he talked and that shit made me want to throw up.

"Man, didn't you learn some fuckin' manners, damn." I sat down in a chair across from him in the office.

"Sorry," he said with his mouth still full.

I shook my head and then let out a sigh. "Ain't shit man."

"Oh, it's something. I can tell." That time he had finally swallowed.

"This fine ass chick named Fanci came in the shop yesterday and man…" I shook my head. "She was everything."

"So, what's the problem?" There was a look of curiosity on his face.

"I ain't even get her number man. You know how it is. Remember that chick Star who was stalkin' me and shit? I met her ass at the shop and after that I vowed to never mix business and pleasure again. I keep it strictly professional."

Travis shook his head. "Okay, so that shit happened wit' Star, but that don't mean every woman you meet at the shop gon' be crazy. Obviously you wanted to get old girl's number or you wouldn't be talkin' about it now."

"Man, you right, but I didn't wanna take that chance. Now I can't get her off my mind. Shit, what's the chances of me runnin' into her again?" I shook my head as I thought about it. Damn, I had really dropped the ball that time.

"More than likely she was feelin' you too and she'll show up at the shop again. I mean, she knows that you don't know how to find her. It's a small world though. If it's meant for you to see her again you will." He took a sip of water from a bottle as I thought about what he said.

"Hmm, this is a big city man. Her showing up at the shop will probably be my only chance of seein' her again. I know that I can't judge all women based on Amil and Star, but damn, they made it so a nigga wanna be out of the game. I'm done playin and shit. I just wanna find the right one you know."

Travis laughed. "Yup. I know man. If you play the game long enough it's gonna get tired. After a while you realize that you wanna settle down. Even the biggest player falls in love eventually. You just at that crossroad my nigga. Right now you tired of playin' the field, but you'll find somebody who's for you. Maybe it's her. Do you at least know her name?"

"Yeah…Fanci. And that name describes her to a tee."

There was a funny look on Travis's face. "You sure you wanna fuck wit' a chick named Fanci?"

I laughed. "I have a weakness for chicks that are high maintenance. Something tells me that she ain't nothing like the chicks I'm used to dealin' wit'. I mean, she just seems so…put together. I mean, baby girl was looking flyy and not even one hair was out of place on her head. Man, she got a tat on her lower calf and my dick was hard the whole time. She had the thickest, sexiest legs I've ever seen. My mouth was watering."

"So my question is why the hell didn't you get her damn number?" He shook his head at me as he wiped his mouth with a napkin. "Well, I guess Operation Find Fanci has started my nig."

A grin broke out on my face. "Man, all I got is her first name. That'll be like finding a needle in a haystack."

"Not really. How many women out there are named Fanci? If that's her real name."

"Oh, she told me that her mother named her that, so it's her real name."

"Maybe she got a Facebook page or something," Travis said as he tapped some keys on the computer.

"Won't hurt to see. I know what she looks like. Shit, I can't forget a face that beautiful."

Travis gave me a funny look. "You really feelin' that chick huh? Damn man. Hope we find her."

I nodded and got up to look over his shoulder as he prowled Facebook for Miss Fanci. "Me too man."

Chapter 3

Fanci

I was participating in my favorite past time, shopping at Phipps Plaza, when I received a notification from my Facebook Messenger. I clicked on the icon that took me to my inbox to read the message.

Devin: Damn, I should've known that a woman as beautiful as you would be married. Just my luck. ☹

At first I rolled my eyes because I thought it was just some random thirsty ass dude, but when I saw that it was Devin my heart skipped a beat. He was the eye candy from the tattoo shop and he had found me on Facebook. My girl Janai was right. He wanted me. I couldn't help but smile.

Me: Oh wow. You found me. ☺

Devin: Yeah, it took me forever. So many Fancys on FB. I finally decided to drop the y and add an i.

Me: Lol. Well, yeah. I am married. That doesn't mean that I'm blind. You're a good looking man.

Speaking of blind, I had almost bumped into the back of somebody. Damn, texting and walking was just as hard as texting and driving. Well, I was really inboxing, but it was the same method. I decided to wait until I was sitting down in my car to continue with our conversation. Suddenly I wanted to talk to him instead of shop. Then I thought about my husband. Was it cheating if I just talked to him? I mean, it couldn't be cheating because it wasn't like we had a physical relationship.

I'd been faithful throughout my marriage, but I'd been tempted several times. None of those times had the attraction been as strong as it was with Devin. The fact that he had found me made it even harder to fight what I felt. I hightailed out of the mall feeling all excited. Like a giddy kid I literally skipped to my white BMW. Once I was seated behind the wheel with my bags in the backseat, I checked my messages again.

Devin: Thank u. When I first saw that you were married I wasn't going to inbox you, but I said fuck it. No harm in us being friends right?

Me: Right. No harm at all.

I knew better than that. We were playing with fire and it was going to do more harm than good if we kept communicating. Still, although we both knew that, there was just something between us. There was some kind of magnetism that neither of us could deny.

> **Devin: To be honest, you been on my mind for the past two days. I can't stop thinking about you. You can't imagine my disappointment right now.**

> **Me: Honestly, you've been on my mind too. I can imagine. I'm there.**

> **Devin: I must admit that I looked thru your pics. He's old enough to be your pops. Not judging but what the hell you doing with him?**

> **Me: Uh, that's kind of personal don't you think?**

> **Devin: Lol. I'm just trying to understand how he ended up with someone as gorgeous as you.**

> **Me: Thank you, but I don't really wanna discuss him.**

> **Devin: I'm cool with that, but one more question about him?**

I sighed.

Me: What's that?

Devin: Did he like your tattoo?

Me: He didn't even notice it.

Devin: Wow. Seriously?

Me: Yeah.

Devin: Damn, is he blind or something? It's been two days and you got a sexy tat on your leg that he ain't seen?

Me: I thought you said you had one question.

Devin: Lol. Right. Well, since we friends now, how about you give me your number.

Me: I'm married.

Devin: I thought you didn't wanna talk about him. I don't.

Me: Lol. Don't do that.

Devin: What?

Me: Tempt me.

Devin: I'm not trying to tempt you. I thought we were gonna be friends.

Me: Yeah right. Do you really think we can just be friends? Shit. Look at you.

Devin: You have all the control Fanci. It's up to you what we be. All I know is I'm feeling you, so if being your friend is all I get to have you in my life so be it. We take this wherever you wanna go.

Me: Oh, the pressure. I'll think about giving you my number. For now we're only gonna be inbox buddies.

Devin: Okay. Fine. For now.

* * *

"You know you're playing with fire right," Janai said giving me a snide look as she cut into her filet mignon.

We were at Longhorn Steakhouse getting our grub on and having a little girl talk. Two weeks had passed since my initial Facebook conversation with Devin. Since then we'd been inboxing one another on a regular and I was thinking about giving him my phone number. We had been on the computer the past couple weeks going back and forth for hours and I wanted to hear his voice. He'd suggested us video chatting, but I didn't want to be more tempted than I already was. Isaac didn't even seem to notice how aloof I was being with him. I guess it wasn't anything different from the norm. We basically just coexisted anyway and I was longing for more.

"We're just friends Janai. I said I was going to give the man my number, not jump in bed with him." Damn, I sure wanted to though.

"Friends?" She rolled her eyes. "Who the hell do you think you're fooling? Friends my ass."

I speared a piece of my salmon, but thinking about Devin had suddenly taken my appetite. Our conversations were getting a lot deeper lately and he was sparking something in me that I hadn't felt in a long time, desire. My sex life had been practically none existent lately and so running my business, shopping and hanging out with my best friend had been my only solace. Suddenly I was longing for some kind of passion and Devin was the blame.

"I'm not satisfied with my husband. I admit that, but that doesn't mean that I'm going to jump into bed with some man that I just met…"

"I thought he was your friend," Janai cut me off.

I rolled my eyes in annoyance. "You know what I mean. He's a friend, but he's a new friend and I don't plan on sleeping with him."

"I know that you're not the type to just fuck some random guy, but at this point he's not just some random guy. He's your friend as you say and that's normally how that shit starts. I'm single, so I don't have to worry about what you're going through girl. I'd hate to be in your shoes right now because I'd be boning Devin on a regular. Fuck Issac. I only have one word for him, divorce. If you're even thinking about cheating you might as well get one." She took a sip of her tea after giving me the tea.

I shook my head. "I feel obligated to Isaac and I can't just leave him like that. If I do it'll prove his bitch of a mother right."

Isaac's mother Iris was the nastiest, judgmental, old bat of a bitch I'd ever met. She hated me since the moment she first laid eyes on me. That was because she wanted him to get back with his first wife and mother of his daughter Megan. She was a lonely old fart who seemed to be in love with her own son. His father had died twenty years ago, so I guess she saw him in her son. It was sick how she doted on a man who was almost fifty.

Iris was a wealthy, seventy five year old white woman who had married a black man despite the racism in the south. I thought a woman who had been in an interracial marriage with a biracial son would be more tolerant, but boy was I wrong. She knew that I came from nothing, so I wasn't good enough for her son. In her eyes I was some young, poor, uneducated hussy from the wrong side of the tracks. Her husband, the late Isaac Moore, was a famous heart surgeon and she was a neurologist who became a professor in her later years. Now she was retired and I guess making my life miserable was her new job.

"That woman is something else. Speaking of the hubby, what is he up to anyway?"

"Spending time with Megan. She'll be graduating from high school in a couple weeks, so he took her car shopping."

"Oh yeah, that's right. It's funny that your step child is only ten years younger than you." Janai snickered.

"Ha ha ha." I rolled my eyes at her and tried to eat a little bit more of my food. Unfortunately my appetite hadn't returned.

"So, what are you going to do?" Janai asked.

"About what?"

She shook her head. "You can't be thinking about living like this for the rest of your life Fanc. You have to leave him. All he does is drink and everybody in his family looks down on you, even his daughter. He does nothing to defend you. You're not happy and it shows. That shit makes you a real bitch that only cares about materialistic shit. I know that Clarine raised you to want the best, but you take that shit to the extreme. I know that it's because you're looking for something. Something is missing and you are not going to find it until you leave that man. You can stand on your own two feet. How many times do I have to tell you that?"

Hmm, if only she knew. Leaving Isaac just wasn't that easy. Of course our relationship started out on the creep tip. At first I flirted with him just because I wanted a good grade in his class. He started responding to my flirting and soon we were sneaking around together. He would mostly take me out of town for our dates and I enjoyed spending his money. I'd never been exposed to the things he had access to and I wanted that lifestyle. In order to have it, I had to agree to his terms. That meant signing a prenuptial agreement. At first I didn't want to do it, but I also didn't want to give up what I'd wanted all of my life.

When I told Isaac that I wanted to start my own business he literally laughed in my face when I told him what kind. After convincing him that it was worth his while, he invested in Orgasma. If I divorced him I wouldn't get shit. Because of his investment he owned seventy five percent of my company. In the event of a divorce I would leave the marriage with only twenty five percent of the company that I had worked so hard to build. Janai didn't know that.

"It's not that simple Nai. I wish it was."

"What do you mean it's not that simple? Divorce him and get half of his shit. I know a great divorce lawyer. He's one of my clients."

"We have a prenup."

Janai almost choked on her baked potato. "You what?" She took a gulp of tea and cleared her throat.

"What the fuck were you thinking?"

"That I had hit the jack pot and I'd be stupid not to agree to it. I mean, it wasn't like any other men in his position were on bended knee asking for my hand in marriage," I explained. "I thought I'd grow to love him you know."

Janai leaned back in her seat and shook her head. "So if you leave him you get nothing?"

I nodded. "Yup."

"Damn, but you have Orgasma though."

I shook my head. "He owns seventy five percent."

"What the fuck!" She shrieked. "Oh my God Fanc. You're fucked."

"I know," I whined. "See why it's not that easy for me to just leave him."

"Um yeah."

"I need a drink."

"Me too." Janai signaled our waitress.

"What can I do for you ladies?" She asked politely.

"Two margaritas please."

"Salt or sugar?"

"Salt. Bring two Patron shots too."

"Okay, coming right up ladies."

"Thank you," we said in unison.

"No problem."

She walked off and Janai gave me a sympathetic look. "What took you so long to tell me that? I'm your best friend."

I shrugged my shoulders. "I felt stupid I guess."

She sighed. "Yeah, that was stupid. You never sign a prenuptial agreement. If he loves you he'll want to make sure you're okay if you two don't make it. It's like he's forcing you to stay with him."

"I guess that's my punishment for getting married for all the wrong reasons. Shit, I'm so horny I'd probably fuck some man to death if I cheat on him."

We both laughed.

"When was the last time you had some good dick?" Janai asked.

"Before I married Isaac. Remember Jamal Grant's fine ass?"

"Hell yeah. Damn boo." Janai's eyes were filled with sympathy. "That was years ago."

"I know. At first Isaac would at least eat me out real good. Now he's too damn drunk to even do that. I mean, you would think he'd try being that he knows I'm much younger than him."

"Right, I mean, how long does he think you're going to be faithful to his ass." Janai rolled her eyes as if she was the one in my situation.

A few minutes later our waitress returned with our beverages. I took a sip of the margarita and then we both downed our Patron shots. Immediately I was feeling a buzz and Devin entered my mind again. The alcohol had given me liquid courage. Not only was I going to give Devin my number, but I was going to see him. I wasn't going to deprive myself any longer. I wanted him and I wasn't going to deny it anymore. At the age of 28 I realized that I wasn't getting any younger. I'd given Isaac too many years of my life and I was tired of being miserable. It was time for me to enjoy my life, even if it was at the expense of my fluke of a marriage.

* * *

"Mmm, it's so good to hear your voice again," Devin said sounding all masculine and sexy.

"It's good to hear your voice too." I was lying in bed wishing that he was beside me.

Instead I was in bed alone because Isaac had passed out drunk on the sofa in front of the television. Not that it mattered being that I didn't want to sleep with him anyway. We hardly slept together anymore lately and although he'd showered with me that night, there were no attempts at us making love. It was like he didn't care anymore about pleasing me. At times I wondered why he didn't divorce me. I guess he didn't want me to be free to be with someone else. He knew that I wasn't going to leave him.

"So, how are you able to talk to me? Where's the husband?" Devin's voice was full of disappointment when he mentioned him.

"He's passed out drunk on the sofa. Don't worry. We have all night to talk. Believe me, he won't be interrupting."

He knew all about Isaac's drinking problem and our lack of a sex life. It made me feel good when he assured me that I wasn't the problem. I knew that I wasn't an unattractive woman, but I was starting to feel some type of way. After all that time he still hadn't noticed my tattoo. I bet Devin would notice anything that was different about me.

"Good, so, tell me about your childhood."

"My childhood?" I didn't really want to talk about that. "Why would you want to know about my childhood?"

"Well, you never talk about it. You mentioned your mom a few times, but nothing about…"

"I grew up not too far from your tattoo shop, so you can imagine what type of childhood I had."

"Hmm, we're about the same age and I moved here when I was in high school. Which one did you go to, because I would've remembered you if we went to the same school."

I laughed. "I ended up getting a scholarship to go to a private school in Atlanta. Janai and I were one of the few students who did."

"Oh okay, I was about to say how the hell had I missed your fine ass. You probably wouldn't have been into a nigga like me though."

I wanted to ask him about his past since he used words like nigga. It was obvious that he wasn't the type of man I would've normally been into. A woman like me probably wouldn't have given him a second thought if Isaac was doing his job as my husband.

"Well, I'm into you now and that's all that matters right?"

"Right," he agreed.

There was silence on the line as I contemplated how to ask him something.

"What's wrong? Why're you so quiet?" He asked.

I cleared my throat. "Nothing's wrong. I was just thinking."

"About?"

"I can tell from how you talk and carry yourself that you haven't always been a square, or maybe you're not a square now. I'm just curious."

He chuckled good-naturedly. "I ain't gon' lie to you Fanci. Once upon a time I wasn't a law abiding citizen and I did some things I'm not proud of for money. I paid my debt to society though and now I'm on the straight and narrow path as far as the law is concerned. I am far from a square though ma. I know how to turn up when need be."

I laughed. It was a breath of fresh air to talk to somebody who could relate to my past. So, I had never been into that street life, but I could relate to his struggle. Growing up without much made us both do things we didn't want to do for money. He had committed crimes and I had married someone I didn't love. For years I turned my nose up at men like him and now I was relating. How the tables how turned. Knowing Devin was bringing me back to earth.

"I really like talking to you Devin. Life has been stifling for me the past few years. I guess I thought having a husband with money was going to make me happy. That's what my mother always told me. She said that money makes the world go round and if I wanted to be happy I needed to make sure I married a man who had lots of it. Don't get me wrong, the money makes me happy. It's just..." My voice trailed off.

"You don't have children with him, so why don't you leave him if you're so unhappy? Is it all about the money? I thought you said you have your own business."

He sounded like Janai, but I decided to keep the prenup to myself for the time being.

"Well, a marriage is supposed to be for better or for worse, so..."

"Do you love him?" Devin asked suddenly.

I let out a loud sigh. "Do we have to keep talking about my marriage? What about you? Why is a man with his own business who looks like you single?"

"Well, I seem to attract the wrong women I guess." I could tell that he was smiling despite the delicate situation. "Never met somebody like you before now, so if you weren't married I probably would be working on not being single anymore."

"Oh really?"

"Hell yeah ma. Really."

Damn, where had that man been my whole adult life? If I had met him years ago, perhaps things would be different. Then again if I had met him years ago, I probably wouldn't have given him the time of day. We talked for hours and fell asleep on the phone. I woke up slobbering on my phone's screen at six am the next morning. Wow. I hadn't done anything like that since high school.

Chapter 4

Devin

"I can't believe that…woman. I do everything for her and my daughter and she still wanna show her ass." I shook my head and waited for Fanci to respond to what I had just told her.

"Wow," she breathed. "She is really an ungrateful ass bitch. No disrespect, but I'm just saying."

"Fuck her. I wanna see you." There, it was out. "I mean, I love talking to you on the phone, but this phone shit ain't enough. I fuckin' want you Fanci. I wanna to see you. Baby, I wanna touch you. I did tell you that the ball's in your court, but fuck that. Shit, I want yo' fine ass. Every single time we talk I have to fight the fact that I want you, but I can't nomore. I know you feel it too ma. Yo' man ain't takin' care of home, but baby girl I'm more than willin' to do what he won't do. Just let me."

There was silence on the line for a good minute, and I felt like maybe I had over stepped my boundaries.

Fanci let out a loud sigh and then asked, "Damn, you're relentless. When?"

My heart started to pound. Did she just ask me when? Oh shit. I did not expect that.

"Shit, tonight, asap baby. I need you," I let out a breath of relief. At least I knew that Amil wouldn't be popping up.

"Okay," she agreed. "What time and where? I mean, you know that we can't..."

"I know baby, I know. Come to my place. I'm in a low ley spot. I just need you right now. Real shit."

I was so pissed off that Amil had taken my child with her and some nigga to South Carolina. It wasn't like I wouldn't have kept my daughter for her to do what the fuck she wanted to do. When she had random men around my child that shit burned me up. I had called her to talk to my baby girl and she was ready to tell me that some nigga named Rob had taken them to Myrtle Beach. What the fuck was wrong with that broad? She wanted me to go upside her head, but I wasn't going to go there. Making me jealous was her motive, but I didn't give a fuck about her. My only concern was Londyn.

"When can you get away ma? I'm aware of your situation and so, I ain't tryna make shit complicated."

She cleared her throat. "I can get away whenever I want to. Text me your address so I can put it in my GPS. Uh, it's four eighteen now. How about eight o' clock?"

That was perfect. It gave me enough time to get myself together and cook something nice for her. I knew that most women liked wine and I already had some Pinot Grigio on chill. Wine wasn't really my shit, but my friend Gina had given it to me in hopes that I'd have a woman over. That shit made me grin. She was on point that time with her meddling ass.

I knew that Fanci was a woman who was used to the finer things in life, so I couldn't half step. I jumped in my Caddie and headed to the nearest Publix. My plan was to cook garlic shrimp with angel hair pasta and make a tossed salad with garlic bread on the side. Of course I didn't know what kind of dessert she liked, but I picked up a strawberry cheesecake anyway and headed back to the crib. After preparing everything, I took a shower got dressed and lit some candles to place on the dining room table. Before I knew it, it was eight o' clock and my doorbell was ringing.

My heart pounded nervously as I headed to the door. I knew that it was Fanci because she had called to tell me when she was about ten minutes away. She was right on time, which wasn't like most black women. I chuckled as I thought about the fact that she must've been just as anxious as me. When I opened the door my eyes almost popped out of my head.

"Damn," I shook my head and took in the view of her with appreciation. "You're lookin' good ma. Real good."

She grinned. "Thank you. You don't look so bad yourself."

"C'mon in." I stepped aside and let my eyes drift over her thick frame in a white, flowing sundress. There were cute little brown, flat sandals on her feet that showed off her pretty toes.

I was thankful that she hadn't covered up those gorgeous legs.

"Mmm, something smells good," she said as she looked around. "Nice place by the way."

"Thanks. Uh, I hope you're hungry. I cooked a lil' something."

She narrowed her eyes at me. "Oh really. Well, I am glad I didn't eat too much before I got here. I figured we'd eat, but I thought you'd...order something."

I couldn't help but mess with her and act offended. "So you didn't think I could cook huh?"

"Well, you know, it's not cool to assume, but..."

I chuckled and grabbed her hand. "It's ok. I understand ma. You probably thought my crib would be junkie and unfurnished like most bachelor pads too. All I gotta say is I think if you keep fuckin' wit' me you'll keep gettin' pleasant surprises. Now, let's go eat."

When she saw the way I had shit all romantically set up in the dining room, there was a look of sheer shock on her face.

"Wow, I didn't expect all of this Devin." She looked up at me with a radiant smile.

The light was dim with the shimmering glow of the candles that were strategically placed on the square, mahogany table. There was a centerpiece made of white lilies and a bucket of ice with the wine chilling in it.

"Have a seat beautiful. Let me serve you."

"You don't have to tell me twice handsome." She sat down and I couldn't help but admire her facial features.

She looked so soft and feminine, but that didn't really seem to match her personality. I could tell that life had hardened her and made her a little judgmental, but meeting me had seemed to kind of make her a little more open-minded. Maybe that was because as much as she tried to run away from her past, having someone around who could relate to her was refreshing.

We made small talk as I fixed our plates and when I placed hers in front of her, she looked up at me with wide eyes again.

"This looks really good Devin. You sure you didn't order this and then got rid of the boxes and bags?"

I shook my head as I laughed with her. "I promise I cooked it. Now looks can be deceiving. Let's just hope it looks as good as it tastes."

She tasted a little and then nodded her head in approval. I could tell by her facial expression that she liked the pasta and shrimp.

"Mmm and it tastes as good as it looks."

I poured us both some wine. "Thank you beautiful. I was hopin' you'd say that."

Our conversation flowed like the wine and it felt right to be around her. Damn, I was so glad that she agreed to see me, so I had to let her know.

"Thank you Fanci."

"No, thank you Devin, for the food and the company. I mean, I have my mom and Janai, but I miss having a man show me some attention, you know? I don't remember the last time my husband fixed a plate for me, let alone cooked for me."

I looked deep into her beautiful eyes. "Well, get used to gettin' served as long as you're around me beautiful."

There was a look of longing in her eyes that matched exactly how I felt. She just stared at me as she shook her head.

"Do you realize how I just took that statement?" Fanci asked after taking a quick sip of wine.

"I probably meant it that way." My eyes dropped to her cleavage.

Damn, even her breasts were perfect. Not too big, not too small. I wondered if she had nice, big nipples. Oh, I hoped she did. A nigga wanted to suck on them…bad.

She smiled and then licked her lips. So fucking sexy. Mmm.

"I've never cheated on my husband."

"And like I said, you don't have to do anything you don't wanna do ma. I just need you to know that I want you. If you don't want the same, that's fine. I'm cool wit' bein' friends. I meant that. I just can't pretend like I don't wanna lay you down right now and taste every single inch of your fine ass. Shit, I bought dessert, but I'd rather have you. Straight up." I wasn't holding shit back.

What did I have to lose? Not a damn thing. I half expected her to get up from her chair and leave my ass sitting there looking stupid. Still, it didn't matter. I knew what the fuck I wanted and a closed mouth never got fed.

"Damn." Her voice was low and breathless. "You're so fine."

She leaned forward and when our lips touched it was like a spark had been lit instantly. "Mmm," I moaned against her lips just as her tongue slid against mine.

If her kisses tasted that sweet I could imagine what the rest of her tasted like. One delicacy in particular was what I really wanted to put my mouth on. My hands were all over her at that point and when I picked her up she didn't protest. So, I took that as an okay to take her to my bedroom and do all of the things to her that she was missing at home. As I walked with her in my arms, we didn't break our passionate kiss. Instead it got deeper and hotter.

Fanci didn't say a word after we separated for me to lay her gently on the bed. I was wondering if she was having second thoughts and I just didn't want her to reject me. There was no way that I wanted to get all into it and then she decided that she didn't want to, so I asked.

"You sure you want this baby?" My eyes were pleading for her not to say no, but if she did, I was going to respect that.

"Yes," she whispered with her soft hand behind my head.

When she pulled me down for another kiss I was all in. I'd never really been one into tongue kissing and spit swapping, but Fanci was doing something to me that I couldn't explain. I pulled away and looked down at her.

"You are so damn sexy Fanci. I'm gonna show you how a real man treats a woman," I whispered seductively.

She sexily bit her bottom lip as she let me remove her dress. I tossed it on the floor and then removed her bra. For the moment I left her panties on. They would be coming off soon too. The entire time I kissed and tasted her delicious skin. Damn, her husband was crazy as hell to not please her. It wasn't like she wasn't attractive.

Maybe there was a side to Fanci I hadn't seen yet that would explain what was happening in her marriage. Right then and there, I didn't give a fuck. All I knew at the moment was I wanted her bad as hell. Whatever else that came with it would come and I'd cross that bridge when I got there.

"Mmm, Devin." Damn that shit sounded like music to my ears.

Her nipples were hard and aroused as I sucked them lovingly. I could tell by her reaction that something so simple had not been done to her in such a long time. How in the hell could a man deprive his woman like that? I didn't give a fuck how old he was, damn, it wasn't like they didn't make Viagra. The old fool was probably cheating his damn self, so I didn't feel a twinge of guilt as my tongue trailed down his wife's body.

I kissed and licked from her head to her toes and she moaned and writhed in pleasure. To say that I was turned on was to say the least. A nigga's dick was rock hard, but her pleasure was my top priority. I had a feeling that she was going to take care of me later if I put it down just right, which I planned to do.

After sucking all ten of her pretty toes, my tongue moved up her leg to her thigh. I could feel her trembling beneath me and when I looked up she had an anxious look on her face. It was like I could read her mind. She was wondering if I was going to finally devour that sweet smelling pussy. Her juices were flowing and my animalistic attraction to her was taking over my senses. Oh, she was about to get her answer. I was definitely going to go in on that shit.

As I stared at it, I had to touch it first. How could I not? Shit, I was a heterosexual, Scorpio who loved a sexy ass woman. It was just slim pickings and so I had learned to control my dick over the years. To be honest, it had not always been that easy. I was a pleaser, but I didn't just go down on anybody. Fanci's fine ass just had some kind of power over me that made me want to do each and every nasty thing that I could imagine to her.

"Ohhh," she whimpered as my pointer finger slowly entered her warm, wetness.

"Damn ma, that shit is tight. Mmm." I dipped down and slowly took her swollen clit into my mouth.

The way her pussy was clenching my finger I wondered if that nigga she was married to had *ever* fucked her.

She arched her back and then let out a deep breath. Baby girl had to exhale. I knew that she needed an orgasm bad as hell. It wasn't hard to tell that her body had been starving for a long time. Well, I was just the nigga to give her nourishment. I had no problem at all doing it, because her pussy was so fresh and tasted so good.

"Mmm mmm mmm…Fanci…" I moaned as I added my middle finger.

Her pussy muscles twitched and squeezed my fingers snugly as I started to lick, suck and slurp on her stimulated clit. She was holding on to my head for dear life and her legs were opened as wide as they could go. Mami was hungry for that shit. She was loving it and my face was wet as hell.

"Devin…yesss…uhhh…keep sucking it baby. Just…like…that. I'm…mmm…I'm…gonna cum…Fuck…ohhh…ohhhh…myyyy…mmmm." Her eyes were on me as she sucked her finger.

"So beautiful…" I whispered and didn't skip a beat as I sucked her clit over and over and over.

She was humping my face and I knew that she was about to cum hard. She grabbed my head and suddenly stopped moving.

"Ahhhh….shit…" she whispered and then a tear fell from her eye and slid down her cheek.

I noticed that she seemed to be holding her breath as her body shook and trembled from her orgasm. Without even thinking about it, I had her clit between my lips and my tongue was doing a dance. Her body jerked again and that time she didn't say anything. She just closed her eyes and rode it out.

"Mmm…" she finally let out as she pushed my face away from her pussy.

"You tappin' out?" I asked with a cocky grin as I grabbed her fat ass cheeks.

"Yes," she whispered. "I want to feel you."

I stared into her eyes. "Whatever you want ma. Like I said before, I'm here to serve you."

After I slid on a condom, I positioned myself on top of her and she willingly spread her thighs for me. She looked up at me in anticipation and I knew that she had a case of the nerves. There I was all throbbing and hard with nine inches of dick about to probe between her legs. I was going to be as gentle as possible, because I knew that she was like a virgin again.

"Let me know if I hurt you," I whispered in her ear and then kissed her neck softly.

"Okay."

She was so wet, so it wasn't really that hard to make my entrance. The thing was, baby girl was so tight that I couldn't get in there like I wanted to.

"Relax baby," I coaxed her as my hands gently caressed her sexy body.

I could feel her open up more for me, so I grinded inside of her juicy, tightness at a slow pace. Damn, it was going to be hard to do, but I was going to take my time. Her pussy was hella good and I had to incorporate the mind over matter tactic. If I didn't I was going to be nutting in less than two minutes.

"Mmm...uhhh...damn Devin..."

She sounded so fucking sexy. Everything about her was pushing me over the edge. Her sexy body, that gorgeous face, the smell of her hair, oh and the pussy on her was magnificent.

"Damn ma, I could stay inside of you forever. You feel like heaven."

Damn, if only she wasn't married. That shit was just my luck. Finally, I had met somebody who was everything that I desired in a woman and she belonged to some other muthafucka. Yet and still, she had a nigga whipped anyway and for once in my life I was willing to share. Well, wasn't that some shit.

Chapter 5

Fanci

It was after twelve when I finally made it to my car with wobbly legs that felt like jelly. I had to call Janai because I was about to burst if I didn't.

"What? You said you fucked Devin? What bitch? Did you just say what I think you said?" She asked all loud and shit.

I was glad she lived alone.

"You heard me. Please don't make me say it again." I could still feel him inside of me and my body felt so damn relaxed from all of those good ass orgasms. That man had definitely served me right and I was officially gone over that "D".

"Oh my God. You really did it. I knew it. The moment you looked at that man I knew you wanted to fuck him."

I sucked my teeth. "Oh please. It's not like I pursued him. He found me."

"Well, you damn sure went for it head on girlfriend," she giggled. "So, details. How was it?"

"Fucking amazing. He cooked for me, the conversation was on point like always and then he told me that he wanted me for dessert. Even if I wanted to say no I couldn't. I mean, shit, I hadn't had any good dick that isn't battery operated in so damn long. Oh my God. His tongue is the truth Nai." My memory was filled with the pleasure he had put down on me. "If I wasn't married I would've spent the night so I could wake up to that big dick in the morning. That man is a master in the bedroom. He put it down Nai. For real."

"Girl bye. You just ain't had no real dick in so long anything would be good to you." Her laughter was contagious.

"Whatever. If I wasn't stingy with the dick I'd tell you to try it out."

"I ain't no microwave bitch, so don't be trying to pass me your leftovers," she shot back.

I laughed hard as hell and noticed just how sore I already was from that good ass session. "Damn. I'm going to be suffering for that shit. My shit's sore as hell already."

"So, how big was it girl?"

I thought about it. It wasn't like I had measured it or anything.

"Uh, all I know is that shit was nice and thick. Wayyy bigger than Isaac, which wouldn't be hard."

"Girl, you seen a ruler before. Estimate."

I laughed. "Maybe eight and a half, nine inches."

"Ohhh damn. Yeah, I bet your pussy lips are all the way down to your ankles right now."

"Good thing Isaac won't be trying to get some no time soon. He'd know for sure that I got some new dick. Shit."

"Fuck Isaac. Hmm. He ain't doing his job and that's what happens. You have to think about it though boo. I know it's good, but there are consequences. Be careful."

I didn't care about the consequences. I wasn't leaving Devin alone. The crazy thing was, I knew that once upon a time I wouldn't have ever fucked with somebody like him. Maybe that was the reason that I was so miserable. It was probably my karma for turning my nose up at men like Devin.

"Oh, I will honey. Believe that."

* * *

When I walked in the house on cloud nine, I was suddenly brought back down by the sight of Isaac sitting there on the sofa. He seemed to be waiting for me, which was odd. I expected for him to be laid out drunk and not giving a damn about what I was doing as always.

"Where the fuck have you been?" He asked looking at me with disdain.

My hair was not all over my head, but I had sweated my do out a little bit. I had a hair appointment early that morning anyway. If he knew any better, or had any form of intuition, he'd know that I'd been out fucking around on him.

"Out with Janai. Why?" I frowned down at him wondering why he suddenly seemed to give a fuck.

"Hmm, you were out with Janai. You and Janai must be lesbians. Every time I turn around you're with her."

I shrugged my shoulders. "And if we were what difference would it make?" With that said I turned around and headed up the stairs.

I'd taken a shower at Devin's and my panties were inside of my purse. I didn't think twice about it being that I didn't think Isaac would be up ready to interrogate me.

Thankfully he didn't follow me, so I undressed and climbed between the covers. I was spent and there was a huge grin on my face as I thought about Devin. Without a second thought I grabbed my phone and sent him a text.

> **Me: Goodnight sexy. I can't wait to see you again.**

I got a response less than two seconds later.

> **Devin: Goodnight beautiful. It will be real soon. Sweet dreams.**

If they were about him they'd damn sure be sweet.

* * *

After my hair appointment I had a one o'clock meeting at Orgasma's headquarters about potentially adding a few more items to our inventory. I got there at about twelve thirty and my Personal Assistant Chloe greeted me with a huge grin on her face.

"Girl, that husband of yours is so sweet. He sent flowers. Is your Anniversary coming up or something?" She asked with a huge grin on her face.

Chloe had flawless cinnamon brown skin, and stood about 5'2 with a small frame. Her hair was cut short and she kept it fierce. She had a pair of wire framed glasses perched on her nose as she followed me to my office.

I was confused. Issac hadn't sent anything to the office for me in almost a year. Hmm, maybe he was suspicious.

"Love you hair by the way," Chloe's voice seemed far away as I noticed the huge bouquet of orange and white roses on my desk. It had to be at least three dozen.

"Thanks," I threw over my shoulder as I looked for a card. There wasn't one. Odd.

My heart pounded in my chest and then my phone rang inside my purse. I reached for it and took a look at the screen.

"Excuse me Chloe. I'll be out in a little while."

She just stood there was a questioning look on her face as I closed the door.

"Hi handsome," I answered with a smile.

"Hey beautiful. You get your flowers?" Devin asked.

I could tell that he was smiling too.

"Yes, they're beautiful. Thank you." I should've known that Isaac hadn't sent them.

"So, what time does your meeting start again?"

"At one."

"How long do you think you'll be? I miss you."

My body suddenly felt flushed and I turned on the small fan that sat on my desk.

"Not long. A couple hours. I miss you too."

"I want to see you again. Why don't you stop by after it's over?"

"Uh, but Devin, we just…"

"It wasn't enough." His voice was sexy and raspy.

"Mmm, I feel the same way, but I don't know…"

"Okay. I know you have to go. Just think about it and if you do decide to come over…bring some of those toys wit' you."

With that said he hung up and I was left to sit there and marinate on that shit.

* * *

Of course I showed up at Devin's door with my bag full of tricks. The intrigue alone was enough to make me decide to just say fuck it and go. Yeah, we'd just had sex the night before, but just like him, I couldn't get enough. I'd never experimented with the toys that I sold with someone else, so I was definitely turned on by the thought.

When he opened the door he didn't say a word. The lust in his eyes said it all as his lips covered mine. He picked me up and tongued me down good as he carried me to the bedroom.

I broke the kiss and asked, "No dinner this time?"

He groaned. "You *are* my dinner. I'll feed you later."

I couldn't help but laugh, but he ended it abruptly with another kiss. After he laid me down on the bed he undressed me and laid down beside me. That surprised me.

"What's one sexual fantasy that you have, but never had a chance to explore?" He asked with his fingers in my hair.

His eyes were on my face and then they roamed over my tempting, naked body. Before I could answer he leaned over and kissed me softly. When he finally stopped kissing me I replied with no reservations. I had never been a prude, but I hadn't really had the chance to experiment sexually. I knew that I was approaching my sexual enlightenment and I wasn't trying to let my good years waste away with Isaac's old lame ass.

"I've always wanted to be ate out and fucked at the same time. I've never explored that fantasy because I'm not into women. I can only see that happening during a threesome and no straight man that I know is going to invite another man into the bed with him."

He smiled down at me with those sexy ass eyes twinkling. "Well, I won't be inviting no niggas in here and I can't literally fuck you and eat you at the same time, but depending on what you got in that bag, I can do something similar. Guess my fingers ain't enough huh?"

I laughed. "Don't get me wrong babe, your fingers are fine, but I have something else for you to use."

I reached for my bag and pulled out a dildo that was about the size of his penis. If he ate me and used that shit at the same time it would simulate my sexual fantasy. There was no doubt in my mind that he was thinking the same thing.

He shook his head and let out a masculine chuckle. "I ain't never fucked a chick wit' a dildo before since I'm well equipped, but I'll do whatever you want baby."

"Don't worry. I'll be getting the real thing later I'm sure."

He nodded looking serious all of a sudden. "Lay back down ma. I got this. Spread those sexy, thick thighs for daddy."

Damn that man turned me on without even trying.

I felt his mouth on me first and then the pressure of him pushing the dildo inside of me. When it was all the way in, stretching me to the limit, I could feel my body tremble. He pushed and twisted that shit against my G-Spot as he sucked and slurped my hardened clit.

"Uhhh…shit…Devin…God!" I screamed as I came faster and harder than I ever had in my entire life.

It was like there had been a double explosion that started deep inside of me and then spread to my overly stimulated clitoris.

"Fuck!" I was out of breath as I scooted away from his hot, steamy mouth.

The dildo was still inside of me, but I couldn't take any more of his lethal ass tongue.

There was a satisfied smile on his face and I could tell that he was feeling victorious.

"You good ma?" He asked as he licked his lips.

Everything he did was so fucking sexy that it should've been illegal.

I shook my head in disbelief as my body shuddered with aftershocks.

"Are you kidding me? That shit was incredible. I have never came so hard in my life."

He reached over and pushed the dildo deep inside of me again. The movement of his wrist made it feel like I was really getting fucked by him. Then his tongue was lashing at my clit again.

"Ohhhh…yessssssss…like that…" I closed my eyes, threw the pussy back at him, and held on to the back of his head as an incredible orgasm slammed into my body again.

I pushed him away again and he stared up at me with dazed eyes. "Your pussy tastes so damn good. It's crazy wet and open right now. You ready for some real dick? Shit, I'm ready for that pussy. Can't wait for that tight ass mufucka to snap 'round my dick like a rubber band." He slapped my ass cheeks one by one.

"I'm ready," I whispered as he kissed me, sharing the essence of my nature.

"What else you got in there?" He asked as he nodded toward my bag.

I smiled slyly as I reached for it. My body was weak as hell from what he had just done to me, but I wanted more. Shit, it was like I was a glutton for his love making. I pulled out a vibrating bullet and he smiled even harder. His sexy eyes narrowed and then his smile faded.

"Turn around."

I did as he said and tooted my ass up in the air.

"Twerk it for me." He slapped each of my ass cheeks again.

My ass bounced as I glanced back at him. When I blew him a kiss I heard him turn the bullet on. He placed it against my already throbbing clit and then entered me slowly.

"Mmm, damn, your dick feels soooo good," I moaned.

"You got me so fucked up over you Fanci," he whispered in my ear.

My entire anatomy tingled and I was having another amazing orgasm in no time.

* * *

"You hungry my love?" Devin asked after shaking me from my slumber.

I looked up at him not realizing that I had fallen asleep. "What time is it? How long was I sleep?"

"It's only five thirty. You ain't been sleep long babe. Relax. C'mon, you need to eat something. You busted enough nuts for the both of us." He grabbed my hand and led me into the kitchen.

I couldn't help but laugh because he was right. We had done all types of shit in every single position imaginable and I was ready to go again. I didn't want him to think that I was some type of freak, so I sat down at the table.

There was a spread of Chinese food in trays and boxes.

"You didn't cook this time huh?"

"Hell nah. Shit, you wore me out. I ordered that shit."

I smiled at him. "I love Chinese food. Well, what I can identify."

He laughed. "Good. I didn't know what you like so I ordered a bunch of shit. Help yourself gorgeous."

"Thank you," I said gratefully because my stomach was grumbling.

After piling my plate with braised chicken wings, shrimp fried rice, steamed broccoli and pepper steak, I dug in like I was famished.

"Slow down before you choke ma."

"I'm starving."

"Hmm, so does that mean I put it down right?" His sexy eyes were on me.

"Yes, it does." I blew a kiss at him and he pretended to catch it.

"Hmm, I wish I could talk to that nigga," he said.

"Who?" I took a sip of the bottled water he had put beside my plate.

"Your husband." He cleared his throat. "I know you don't wanna talk about him, but I'm dumb founded right now. Shit. There's no way in hell I could lay beside a woman who looks like you, with a body like yours without twisting you up every night. I mean, damn." He shook his head. "I just don't get it. I mean, I personally know how good you feel. I'm addicted to yo' ass. He got you and don't know the first thing to do wit' you. Damn shame. What a waste."

"Wish I had met you first." It came out of my mouth without me even thinking about it.

"If you had met me first nothing would've came of it. I wasn't in the position then that I'm in now. I was a thug and you wouldn't have wanted that. I know. I can tell that you're used to the lifestyle that nigga's provided for you. Look at you. You rock Gucci and Red Bottoms. I know that you wouldn't have ever fucked wit' me back then. This

is our time ma. It was meant to happen this way."
He grabbed my free hand and kissed it.

I didn't know what to say, so I didn't say
anything. Instead I continued to feed my face. When
he talked about Isaac it made me feel some type of
way. It was like I wanted him out of the way so that
I could see where things could possibly go with
Devin. Still, I didn't want to let go of the lifestyle
that Isaac provided for me. I was stuck between a
rock and a hard place, but I wasn't willing to let go
of that "D" on the side either. Hell no. It was just
too damn good and his personality wasn't bad
either. Not to mention the fact that the man was
sexy as hell and fine. Damn, I was fucked.

Chapter 6

Devin

After we ate we moved to the sofa in front of my 72 inch flat screen to see what was on. I had pulled out two iced cold Coronas from the fridge and rolled a fat ass joint.

"Damn, I haven't smoked weed or drank a beer since my college days," Fanci said after taking a sip.

"Really, why?" I asked. "It ain't like you gotta take a piss test."

"Well, the hubby doesn't think either of them are lady like so…"

"Fuck him." I passed her the joint. "I don't see nothin' wrong wit' a woman smokin' a lil' tree and sippin' on a beer every now and then. It ain't like you smokin' crack or some shit."

"Right," I agreed. "That's what I said at first, but eventually I ended up letting him dictate what I should or should not do. Janai smokes though."

"You mean to tell me that you don't smoke with your best friend?" I couldn't believe that. I would think that Fanci was strong minded enough to do her own thing regardless.

"I guess he convinced me that weed is…hood…and I was trying to get away from that…" Her voice trailed off as she took a pull from the joint.

I watched attentively as she inhaled and held it in for a while before blowing the smoke out. She didn't even choke, instead she hit it again and again before passing it back. When she closed her eyes I watched her in silence. Neither of us said a word. I just enjoyed the blessing of her beauty. Deep down inside I knew that I wanted her for myself, but what could I do. She wasn't trying to leave that fool she was married to.

"That's some bullshit. I know all types of people who smoke weed. Even doctors and lawyers," I said.

"True. Just the smell alone brings back memories of carefree times." She leaned back on the sofa and I softly kissed her neck.

A loud knock at the door interrupted the moment. Damn, I was trying to get a little bit more of that good good before she left. She gave me a look. "You expecting company?"

"No." I continued to kiss her neck and the knocking got louder.

"Uh, are you going to get the door, or pretend like you don't hear that shit?"

I sighed and reluctantly stood up from the sofa. It was still early, so maybe Trav had decided to stop by. If he had called first I had no clue, since I hadn't checked my phone in hours. When I looked through the peep hole and saw Amil standing there it infuriated me. Why the hell did she keep popping up at my spot? I decided not to open the door. Maybe she'd just leave.

Shit, I knew better. I was sure that she saw my car and Fanci's car in the visitor's parking spot. She was aware that I had someone over. I didn't expect for her to make it back from her rendez-vous to South Carolina so soon. Then I thought about it. She didn't have Londyn with her, so I went ahead and opened the door. Besides, who I had over at my crib was none of her damn business.

"Where the fuck is my daughter?" I asked with an attitude.

She stood on her tip toes and tried her best to look over my shoulder. "She's wit' Laila." That was her sister, but something told me that she was lying. "Who the fuck you got over here? I saw that Beemer out there."

"Don't worry 'bout who is over here. Why the fuck you here? You gon' stop poppin' up like you pay bills in this bitch. I pay all yo' damn bills and I still don't pop up at yo' spot! I'm pissed because you took my child wit' you and some nigga to South Carolina and shit. You know how I feel about you takin' her 'round them niggas you fuck wit'. If somethin' happens to my child that's gon' be yo' ass! I don't give a fuck about what you do or who you do it wit', but I give a fuck about Londyn!" I was so pissed that I had almost forgot that Fanci was there.

"Oh, so you don't give a fuck about me? Where that hoe at?" She was trying to push past me to get in, but she wasn't strong enough.

I shoved her gently, stepped out into the hallway and closed the door behind me. "Just leave Amil. Straight up."

"I ain't goin' nowhere! Who the fuck is the bitch Devin? Huh? It's like that now? You tryna move on and shit? What the fuck did I tell you muthafucka? Huh?" Her finger was in my face as she gave me a threatening look. "Didn't I tell you I'm gon' handle any bitch you fuck wit'?"

I pushed her hand away. "Bye Amil. Go get my damn child."

"Fuck you nigga!" She hissed. "I ain't goin' no fuckin' where. You gon' have to call the fuckin' cops to get me to leave."

My frustration showed as I sighed. "I can't believe yo' ass. You was just fuckin' some nigga and now you tryna regulate what the fuck I do?" I shook my head. "Wow. You're unfuckingbelievable!"

"Tell that bitch to come out here so I can go ahead and get her ass whoopin' over wit'! I bet she ain't got shit on my fine ass! You know you want me nigga! I don't even know why you playin'! Come out here bitch!" She screamed. "Bring yo' hoe ass out here and face me like a real woman bitch!"

I put my hand over her mouth. "Shut the fuck up. Shit. What the fuck's wrong wit' yo' crazy ass? Damn."

After a few seconds I let her go.

"I'm still in love wit' you muthafucka. That's what's wrong wit' me." Tears filled her eyes, but I felt nothing. "Come out here bitch!" She yelled even louder that time.

I grabbed her around her waist. "Fuck! Will you just leave? Damn!" I yelled feeling even more aggravated. There was no way that I was going to let them fight, so I just hoped that Fanci would stay inside while I handled Amil.

Something told me that she could hear everything that was going on outside of the door. If she was anything like I thought she was she was going to come out sooner or later. Instead of letting that happen I literally carried Amil kicking and screaming to her car.

"Put me down nigga! I'm gonna kill you and that bitch! I'm gon' get her license plate number and stalk the fuck out of her ass and then I'm gonna shoot that home wrecking bitch in the fuckin' face!"

Once we were outside and I spotted her car, I made my way over to it without saying a word. At that point I had her slung over my shoulder and she was punching me in the back hard as hell as she talked shit.

"Fuck you Devin! I hate you! How the fuck you gon' play me for some random ass bitch! I hate you! I'll make sure you don't ever see Londyn again, 'cause I'm gonna kill you and that hoe!"

I put her down on her feet when I made it to her car. "You finished yo'? 'Cause I ain't got time for yo' bullshit."

"Yeah, 'cause yo' ass entertainin' some bitch!" There was an evil ass smirk on Amil's face as she stared at me. When she reached in her purse I assumed that she was getting her keys. Maybe she had finally came to her senses and was going to leave peacefully. When she pointed a black handgun in my face I didn't even flinch. I should've known that she wouldn't just leave.

"For real ma? You gon' point a gun in my face? The gun I bought you for protection." I shook my head in disbelief. "You shoot me who gon' pay yo' bills ma? Who gon' take care of Londyn? Not them lame ass mufuckas you be fuckin' wit' and you know that."

Tears filled her eyes and then slid down her cheek. "I can't stand the thought of you bein' wit' somebody else. Why don't you want to be wit' me? What the fuck is so good about that bitch?"

My voice was calm as I tried to reason with her. "It's broad daylight and you got a gun in my face. Look around Amil. It's mufuckas out here and shit. This ain't the hood ma. You don't think somebody's gon' call the cops?"

She looked around with a frantic look on her face. Obviously she didn't think about what she was doing. Her emotions were fucked up and I got that, but it would never work out between us.

"Put the gun away and leave before shit get outta hand."

She reluctantly put the gun back in her purse and then wiped her tears away. Suddenly she was back to being a bad ass.

"Fuck you Devin! I'm gon' get that hoe. Just know that shit!"

"I ain't goin' in 'till you leave."

She glared at me maliciously as she opened the door and got in behind the wheel. "I'm gon' leave mufucka, but you better believe that this shit's just beginnin'. Consider yourself warned."

I just stood there as she put on some dark, oversized shades, turned the key in the ignition and drove off. After making sure that she was long gone, I made my way back inside of my apartment building. Damn, I knew that it was going to be some more drama with Fanci. There was no way that she was going to let that shit fly. More than likely she was probably turned off by my baby mama drama.

When I walked inside of my apartment Fanci stood up with her pocket book on her shoulder.

"Are you good?" She was seemingly concerned, but it was obvious that the scene Amil had caused made her want to leave.

I nodded. "I'm straight. I'm sorry yo'. Uh, that was…"

"Amil, your child's mother. I figured that. No need to apologize, but I heard every word that hoe said. It took everything in me not to come out there and fire her ass up. I'm a lady though, so I held it together." She sighed and the moment felt awkward as hell. "I'm going to go ahead and leave now."

I walked over to her and wrapped my arms around her waist. "Okay, but don't let what happened change things between us."

She looked at me with eyes full of regret. Damn, I hated that look.

"Things are already complicated enough without your baby mama drama Devin." She pulled away from me. "I'll call you."

I nodded, but didn't say anything to protest. She was right. Our "situationship" was complicated as hell. Before walking out she didn't even bother to look back at me. There wasn't even a goodbye kiss. Just like that Amil had ruined everything. In my mind I was working toward getting the woman of my dreams. The fact that she was married was just a small obstacle. If I played my cards right I could get her to leave that nigga. No, I wasn't afraid of her being unfaithful to me, shit *I* planned to keep her satisfied.

"Can I walk you to your car?" I asked hoping to get a kiss.

"I can make it to my car just fine. Thank you."

The door closed behind her and I plopped down on the sofa in defeat. Someway, somehow I had to get her back in my good graces. I planned to give her time though. I would wait until she called me and then I would put things into motion. It was my mission to have her all to myself by any means necessary.

* * *

Fanci

I could not believe that ghetto bird bitch had showed up at Devin's acting like that. What the fuck had he ever seen in her to make him lay down with that hoe and make a child? From the way she acted in those few minutes, I could imagine that the shit had to have just been physical. Maybe she could suck a mean dick, I didn't know, but she was showing out over his ass. Yeah, the dick was good, but damn hoe, have some class.

As I shook my head and pressed the button to unlock my car door, I suddenly heard the sound of gunshots. They were close as hell, so I jumped in my car and got down low between the seat and steering wheel. My first thought was it was that bitch Amil. She was a hood ass heifer and so I figured she had access to a gun. Was that bitch trying to kill me? Was it that serious?

After a few more shots there was silence and then the sound of a car pulling off. Unfortunately I wasn't willing to look up and see what the car looked like. I wasn't trying to get shot up if she had reloaded. So, I stayed where I was for a good fifteen minutes before finally sitting up in my seat. My first thought was to call Devin, but I had to get the fuck up out of there. There were a few people outside and I was sure that they had seen something. Instead of asking them I headed on home. Shit, I knew that it was Amil, but thankfully I was alive and none of her bullets had hit my car. None shooting bitch.

* * *

"Your crazy ass baby mama shot at me!" I yelled into the phone. "But I'm good though."

"She did what? Fuck!"

"So, that's all you gotta say? I know you heard the gun shots and that's why you're calling."

He sighed. "I did hear them and that was my first thought."

"And why would that be your first thought Devin?"

"She pulled out on me."

I was appalled. "So why the fuck didn't you tell me that? Is that why you asked me if you could walk me to my car?" It all made sense, so why didn't he just walk me to my car anyway?

"What if I'd been killed Devin? Did you think about that?" I shook my head. Maybe he wasn't worth it. Shit was out of hand already and I'd rather have the peace of my worthless ass marriage. At least I was used to it.

"I'm so sorry Fanci. I thought she was gone ma. I'd feel like shit if something happened to you. I'd be fucked up."

He sounded genuine, but at that point I didn't give a damn. "I'm going to fall back Devin. It was fun, but I have my own issues to deal with. Getting shot at was not on my "to do" list today." My tone was sarcastic, but I didn't care. That was why I didn't fuck with hood dudes in the first place.

"Well you need to handle that bitch. My husband isn't trying to kill you." I was pissed the fuck off.

There I was having a good ass time for once and then all of a sudden there that bitch was causing havoc. Out of all of the shit I'd gone through with Isaac's ex-wife, it was nothing compared to what Amil had done. All Lorraine did was talk shit on the low. I wasn't afraid of her doing anything to me. That heifer Amil had me wondering what she was capable of.

"I'm gonna call you back ma."

He hung up and I thought about calling Janai, but didn't. I wasn't in the mood to hear her say that she had told me that there would be consequences. It wasn't like I didn't already know that something like that would happen. I just didn't think the man I was fucking would have a psycho ass bitch in his life like Amil. The worst case scenario that I could think of would've been a fight.

I was down for that, but damn, was my life hanging in the balance over some dick?

And it was some damn good dick too, but I had left the hood to escape the gun play. Was creeping around with Devin worth it? My mind suddenly drifted to the wild, crazy sex we'd just had a few hours ago. It trumped all of the bullshit that had happened afterwards. Damn, that man really knew how to push the boundaries when it came to freakiness. He would put his mouth anywhere, even between my ass cheeks. I especially loved the way that shit felt. Of course I didn't use any dildos on him, but I did hold one of those vibrating bullets against his balls and he loved that shit. When he came he literally sounded like a bitch with all of the mmms and ahhhs. I felt so powerful. My husband had never ever made me feel that way. He was the one who had all of the power throughout our relationship.

Then I thought about Amil again and the fact that she had actually shot at me. I was glad that she couldn't shoot, or did she intend to shoot me? If she did I wouldn't have been on my way home. Instead I would've been in the morgue stuffed in a body bag with a tag on my toe. Not only that, but I would be known as the woman who had been murdered while cheating on her husband. The story would probably end up on a show on the ID

Channel. With all of the drama going on something told me that the bitch just thought she was scaring me away from Devin. If she wanted to shoot me I was sure that she could have.

All I could do was hope that Isaac was asleep, or that he wouldn't ask me any questions about where I had been or what I'd been doing. He had already called me over a dozen times in the past few hours. It was like men could sense when their woman was up to something. Shit, before I was getting my back banged out by Devin he hardly said two words to me.

*　*　*

"Oh shit," Isaac said when I walked through the door. "Two nights in a row."

I rolled my eyes and headed upstairs without saying a word. To my dismay he followed me and when he got close to me I didn't smell alcohol or tobacco. I wondered if I smelled like that strong ass weed I'd been smoking with Devin.

"So you was with Janai again?" He asked on my heels. "I thought you had a meeting today at work…"

I cut him off. "I did have a meeting and then I went to a bar and had some drinks with Chloe and Juan."

Juan was the manager of Orgasma and I loved his gay, Mexican ass. Isaac didn't know Juan and Chloe like that. He loved the money that Orgasma generated, but in his eyes I was in the smut business and he wanted no parts of it. He made me keep it a secret, so nobody in his family knew about my business. I had told my mother all about it though. My mom only had one sister named Frances. I didn't have siblings and my grandparents died before I was twenty, so our family unit was very small.

So why didn't you answer my calls or at least call me to tell me where you were," he snapped. "I *am* your husband."

I shook my head and let out a sharp breath. "I don't understand you Isaac. You asked me to marry you, but after seven years you act like I'm some burden that you don't want to deal with. Now all of a sudden you want to pretend like you give a damn about me. Forgive me if I don't know how to respond to that."

"Well, you've never stayed out so late two nights in a row. I'm starting to wonder what you're really up to. Are you cheating on me?" His eyes were unreadable. I didn't know if he was just jealous, or genuinely hurt.

"No, but would you blame me if I was?" I shook my head and took off my clothes. "It's not like you pay me any attention anymore."

He watched me undress and his eyes were filled with lust as I slid my white, silk nightgown on. Oh hell no. He was not about to get any of my goodies. Something told me that he was about to try to, but after having sex for hours with Devin, there was no way.

"I know that I haven't really been in a…romantic mood lately and I'm sorry." He sat down on the bed and rested his head in his hands. "I just…you know…I'm…"

"Don't worry about it Isaac. I'm just fine." With that said I turned the lamp off.

There was silence in the room and then he let out an agitated grunt. "So, I try to do something different and this is what I get."

"I'm tired Isaac," I sighed. "It's been a long day and I just want some sleep."

He just didn't know the half and I wondered if Devin had called my back. If only he'd just leave the room so that I could check my phone. Damn him. I was wondering if Devin had talked to that crazy bitch or not. As much as I didn't want to leave him alone, if he didn't handle her I would have no choice in the matter. I was feeling him, but not that damn much. He was fine, but not that damn fine.

Suddenly Isaac undressed and got in bed with me. Before I could say a word his arm was around me and his lips were pressed against my neck.

"I love you Fanci. I've just been stressed out lately. I'm working on the drinking. I do listen to you baby, whether you know it or not."

My back was turned to him, so he didn't see me roll my eyes in annoyance. Why didn't he just go away so that I could talk to Devin like I really wanted to? I wanted to know what that hoe Amil had said and what he planned to do to handle her. When we talked I was going to mention him going with me to press charges against her.

I faked a yawn and stretched. "Okay baby. I'm really tired. Can we just go to sleep now?"

Honestly sleep wasn't anywhere near what I really wanted to do. I was wired and feeling the need to get away from my husband. Maybe a vacation was exactly what I needed to clear my mind and relax.

"Okay," he whispered before kissing my cheek.

His beard's stubble lightly scratched my skin and the familiar feeling made me feel nostalgic. There was a time when I was really cared for him, but those feelings were gone. They had died an awful death and it was too late to raise them from the ashes. It didn't matter what Isaac did to try. It was just too damn late to save us.

Chapter 7

Devin

"What the fuck made you do some dumb shit like that yo'?" I asked Amil when she finally answered her phone two hours after the first time I called.

I didn't bother to call Fanci because I knew that she was in her feelings and shit. Instead I waited until I could reach my crazy ass baby mama. I hated to call her that, but she was falling right into that stereotype. She'd cheated on me several times, which was probably my karma for doing the same thing early in the relationship. By the time I was ready to get serious, she was ready to get even. I couldn't let that go and she couldn't let go of the fact that it was over between us.

"I ain't do shit," she said sticking to her claim of innocence.

"It ain't no fuckin' coincidence that somebody was shootin' when Fanci left my crib. You did point a gun in my face. Why the fuck should I believe you right now?" I let out a sigh of frustration.

"Well, those damn gunshots could've came from anywhere. If I had shot my gun that bitch would be dead. Did she fuckin' see me shoot at her?" She challenged me.

"I'on know what she saw Amil, but I do know you. Where the fuck my daughter at?" I was tired of dealing with her childish bullshit. If I could just get my daughter I wouldn't have to.

"She's sleep in her bed nigga. Where you think she's at?" Amil had an attitude like I had just busted my gun at a nigga that she was fucking with.

Honestly, I wanted to at times because of Londyn, but unlike Amil, I refrained from doing reckless ass shit. All that would do was make the situation worse. We were adults who were also parents and she really needed to start making mature decisions. Unfortunately I had a child with a woman who did not have the motherly instinct. Instead she used our child as a pawn to make my life as miserable as possible. I loved Londyn, but I really resented the hell out of her mother.

It was crazy because before our daughter was born, I didn't see her in such a bad light. Honestly, back then, before life was so serious, that crazy shit that she did turned me on. I think once I became a father I wanted something different. Amil was a bad example for our daughter and I didn't want her to have so much influence over her when she was old enough to understand what was really going on.

"Look Amil, I'm really feelin' like you need some consequences to come from your actions so you can learn. What if I reported you to the police and shit? You know these mufuckas 'round here ain't used to hearin' no gunshots that close. The cops came through askin' questions and of course I said I ain't know shit."

She laughed. "You sound stupid as fuck. Do you hear yourself? I'm the mother of your child? Would you really turn me in to the cops for something that you ain't even sure that I did for a fact? Not only that, but you gave me the gun. Even if I admitted that I did that shit, which I didn't, I would have to let them know that you were the one who gave me the gun. You are a felon who's on parole and you're not supposed to have a fire arm. What if I tell them about the .45 and the nine milli that you got at yo' crib? How 'bout that nigga? Think before you threaten me. I ain't some stupid ass, no street sense havin' hoe like that bitch you fuckin'. What's her name? Fanci?" Her laugh was wicked. "Fuck that hoe. She ain't all that and she really ain't gon' be shit when I'm done wit' her ass."

"I'm warnin' you Amil…"

The sound of a click and my phone returning to the home screen let me know that she had hung up. I called her back and it was clear that she didn't want to talk about it anymore, because she kept sending me to the voicemail.

"Fuck!" I yelled and threw my phone into the wall.

It shattered on the hard wood floor in pieces and I didn't even give a damn. I was so damn mad that I just left it there and decided to pour myself a glass of Svedka Vodka before heading to bed. Life had always been complicated and I was usually able to go with the flow, but lately shit was getting out of hand.

As much as I wanted Fanci, I knew that I couldn't have her. I couldn't expect for her to leave her husband for me. She barely even knew me and even if she did, I couldn't provide for her like he did. I knew that she owned her own business, but if it was that easy for her to leave her husband, I was sure that she would have done it already. Shit, they didn't even have any kids, so I didn't really understand why she stayed.

Why did I expect for her to leave though? Although the sex was hella good, it wasn't like we'd known each other long. Honestly, with child support, and helping Amil out, I wouldn't be able to provide equally for Fanci. As I turned the shower on, I suddenly felt a weird feeling come over me. It was like a sign that something even worse was about to happen. I shook my head wondering if Fanci was still willing to deal with me. As much as I knew that our relationship was a recipe for disaster, it was just some magnetic force that made me want her. The desire to call her came over me, but then I remembered that I had broken my phone. Damn!

* * *

Two whole weeks had passed without me talking to Fanci. I had to get a new phone and so I had lost my contacts. The dude at T Mobile reminded me that I needed to save my contacts under my Gmail account so that wouldn't happen again. Even when I attempted to contact her on Facebook she ignored me. She had even unfriended and blocked me.

Amil was thrilled to think that her threat on Fanci's life had worked. She had been stalking my crib to see that she hadn't been there since. When she called me laughing about my girl dumping me it just made me want to see Fanci more. The more time we spent apart the more I wanted her. I wondered if she was missing me too, but it was obvious that she didn't because she hadn't called me. Maybe she and her husband had worked it out.

That thought alone infuriated me. Shit, what the hell could I do about it other than let it go?

"You good? Your next appointment is gonna be here in twenty minutes. Perk up man," Gina said with her lips poked out mockingly. "You're lookin' like a lil' bitch right now."

"I'm straight G, just tired as hell. That's all."

"Whatever nigga. Travis told me all about your women problems and I said women for a reason." She shook her head. "That damn Amil needs her ass whooped for real. That's all the fuck I gotta say."

"Yeah, well I'll go to the pen if I whoop her ass. You gon' do it for me?" I asked with a smile on my face to downplay it because I knew that she would.

Gina had been wanting to beat Amil's ass for years and the feeling was mutual. Amil's jealous ass swore up and down that I was fucking Gina, but she was really only my friend. We'd been close seen the first day I moved to Decatur and although she was sexy as hell, I respected our friendship.

"Just say the word and it's done. You know I can't stand that bitch. Never could," she hissed with her hands on her thick hips.

Gina was not a small chick at all. At 5'10, she weighed a solid 185 pounds. Baby girl was stacked, but I always saw her as a sister. At first I wanted her, but she put me in the friend zone quick and I had stayed there. That was a good thing because she had been the only consistent woman in my life since my mother's absence. For once I hadn't fucked up a relationship that I had with the opposite sex.

"Nah man, I'll handle Amil. You know I got that shit."

She flashed a sarcastic smirk at me. "You think? Honestly, I don't. You have always given that gold diggin' hoe everything she wants. It's like she got some kinda power over you. True, she's Londyn's mama, but do she really deserve all of the extra perks? How could you ever be with another woman if you're spendin' every dime on her? That hoe won't even work at a fuckin' pie shop. It's ridiculous Devin and you know it. It's like because she bore your child she thinks she's royalty. Shut that hoe down, or I will. Straight like that."

I sighed. "Look Gina, that's my business and my life. Okay."

She nodded and threw her hands up for emphasis. "I'm done with it. I'm just gonna sit back and watch the shit hit the fan. Don't call me when you need somebody to help clean it up."

I shook my head not believing that threat for a second. Gina was always there when I needed her. "Just let me know when my next appointment gets here. Who is it again?"

She pressed some keys on the computer and then narrowed her eyes at the screen.

"I don't know. It's shaded out, but there's no name." There was a confused look on her round, honey colored face.

"Damnit. You gotta do better G…"

"Umm, hold the fuck up…"

The sound of the chime from the door opening halted our disagreement and we both forced fake smiles on our faces. I hoped that whoever it was couldn't sense the tension in the air. When I looked back I noticed that it was some strange white man.

"I'm Phillip. I got a one thirty," he said in a monotone voice.

Although my tattoo shop was in the hood, I got all types of clientele from all over. My work and my other artists work was unparalleled, so word got around. Plus my website was the shit and I often did celebrity tattoos and they would shout me out. The plan was to move Tats and All Dat to a location closer to Buckhead. Then the big bucks would really start rolling in.

"Oh okay Phillip. Who is your appointment with?" Gina asked getting back to professional mode real fast.

"I'm here for Devin," he said pointedly.

I spoke up. "Well, that's me. Do you know what you want?"

He nodded. "Yeah man. I want something custom. I heard that you good with that."

It was clear by the way he talked that he was influenced by Black culture.

"A'ight. Well, let's go on back so we can come up with something."

"Okay," he nodded and followed me.

I had to put my feelings aside for the moment. My business and my child were my top priorities. It was mind over matter and I had to remind myself that the most important girl in my life was still around. I would do anything for Londyn and she was all that mattered to me. Still, in the back of my mind there Fanci was front and center.

* * *

When I finally got home that night I stalked Fanci's friend Janai's Facebook page and found out that they were in Miami. Janai wasn't my Facebook friend, but her page wasn't private, so I could see her posts. According to her they only had three more days before returning to Georgia. There were pictures of them on her page and I couldn't help but admire how good Fanci looked in her two piece bathing suit.

Then it hit me. I had to do what I had to do to get her to deal with me again. If there was any chance of her leaving her husband, I had to show her that I was willing to fight for her. I hurriedly searched for a flight to Miami. There was no way that I was going to let Fanci just slip away like that. There was just something about her that kept me wanting more and a nigga like me just didn't give up.

* * *

Fanci

The past two days in paradise were exactly what I needed. Isaac and I had finally had an intimate moment a few days after his attempt to make some type of connection with me. Of course my mind was on Devin the whole time and I didn't enjoy it, but at least Isaac had made an effort. After giving it a lot of thought I decided to just let things go with Devin. His nutty ass ex helped me make that decision. Our little fling was fun while it lasted, but it was time to move on.

Of course I thought about him too, but I knew that leaving him alone was for the best. At first I was hell bent on keeping him around, but at the expense of my life that didn't seem as appealing anymore. All I had to do was let Isaac know that I just needed to getaway and that was why I was never home. He suggested that I take advantage of the time share that he had in Miami since he had to work. I called Janai and asked her if she wanted to go with me and she obliged.

There I was enjoying the glow of the late afternoon sun with a hot ass baby blue bikini on. My objective was to get a golden tan as I sipped on a fruity concoction that was in a coconut. Mmm, it was so refreshing and I was starting to get a buzz.

"So, what's on the itinerary for today?" I asked Janai as I closed my eyes.

I was lounging lazily on a huge, bright yellow beach towel. Damn, I loved what money could do. If I was broke like back in the days I'd be stuck in Decatur where there were no damn beaches. That lifestyle was the pits.

The only reason that I had gone to college was to find a husband. My mother had constantly told me how important it was for a woman to marry a successful man.

"You see where dealing with a no good, broke ass man will get you," she often reminded me when I was younger. "Look at me."

I constantly tried to reassure her that I loved her no matter what and I was proud of the woman that she was. A lot of mothers out there, like Janai's, had succumbed to drugs and the lure of the streets. My mother on the other hand held down a job and sometimes did things that she didn't want to do with other men to give me the best. She never used drugs, drank or smoked cigarettes. The only vice she had was making sure that she took good care of me. It was like she was obsessed. In my mind she was trying to make up for my deadbeat father not being around.

Janai's voice broke through my thoughts. "It's up to you, shit, I've been planning everything since we got here. Now it's your turn missy." She was also sipping on an alcohol laced drink, but hers was in a martini glass with a little pink umbrella floating in it.

The picturesque sight of the sunset had put me at ease and all I wanted to do was relax. We'd been running non-stop since our plane landed two days ago and I was too exhausted to do anything else.

"Well, to be honest with you, I don't want to really do anything but get wasted. Shit, we need to find some good weed."

Janai snickered. "What? You want to smoke some weed? Where did that come from?"

I smiled slyly. "I smoked a joint the last time I was with Devin. I hadn't been that relaxed since our crazy college days. To deal with my life I need something."

"Girl, your life ain't all that bad. You got your health and you're still young. You can divorce Isaac and still make it. I just don't understand you."

I sat up and glared at my best friend. "Yeah, I'm young and I have my health, but damn bestie, cut me some slack here. I told you about my..."

"Fuck his money Fanci. Money ain't everything," Janai snapped.

I rolled my eyes at her. "That's easy for you to say."

"Why? Because I make my own? I never understood why you married Isaac. My mom didn't raise me like yours did, so I always knew that it was all about me, myself and I. I never thought to depend on a man for shit. If you didn't think that way Fanci, you'd be a much happier person. I love you and I want to see you happy. You're not happy." Tears filled her eyes and I had to look away from her to keep from crying.

Janai and I were so close that she felt whatever pain I felt.

I cleared my throat. "I signed the damn prenup because I thought that over time he'd change it. My stupid, young, naïve ass thought he would eventually love me enough to trust me. I guess getting married for all of the wrong reasons backfired on my ass."

She reached over and gave me a much needed hug. "I'm sorry for being so judgmental Fanc. I just don't want you to make the huge mistake that a lot of women make by being stuck in relationships they don't want to be in. This is not the old days. We don't have to do that shit anymore. I got your back. Do you have a copy of your prenup? I'm sure there's a way around that shit.

There has to be a loophole and maybe you just haven't read all of the fine print. I know how you are."

I laughed to keep from crying. "Yes, I do have a copy. I'll give it to you when we get home."

She nodded. "Now, there will be no more talk about that damn husband of yours. Let's enjoy our time here."

"And his money," I added.

She slapped me a five as we laughed.

"So, have you talked to Devin?" She asked.

"Why?" I shot back.

"Umm…" She seemed shocked by my tone, which she should not have been.

"No, I haven't. I don't think I should." My voice was less confrontational.

"Hmm," she simply said.

"I don't want to talk about him either."

"I know, but all I have to say is that man can't control what his baby mama did. Now, I know for a fact that when you were dealing with him you seemed happy. Happier than you've ever been." Her voice cracked. "Although I know that the circumstances were wrong, I was happy for you."

"His child's mother tried to kill me," I pointed out with a shocked look on my face.

"Did she really, or was the hoe trying to scare you?"

I rolled my eyes. "Does it matter? She shot a gun when I was around and Devin obviously didn't turn the hoe in to the cops, so…"

"So you…"

"Leave it alone Nai."

She sighed. "Okay, but…"

"I'm done talking about Devin," I snapped.

My eyes were closed again.

"Oh, really?" I heard a familiar voice ask behind me.

My eyes popped open. "What the fuck?" I shot up and looked back.

There Devin was standing right behind me. Damn, he looked like he belonged on the set of a movie, or at a photoshoot for a magazine spread. He was silver screen handsome, but what the hell was he doing in Miami. I looked over at Janai and she had a guilty ass look on her face.

"I'm gonna kill you," I said under my breath to her.

It was clear that she had something to do with him being there.

"Why?" She asked playing dumb.

"Uh, can we talk please?" He asked me with a humbled looked on his face.

I was instantly pissed. "About what? Why did you come here? I was ignoring you for a reason."

He sighed. "I'm sorry about what happened baby...Fanci."

I was glad that he corrected himself, because I was just about to.

"Uh, I guess I'll leave you two alone to talk," Janai threw in before hurrying away.

That heifer had set me up. What the fuck kind of friend was she? Every time I turned around she had me involved in some crazy ass shit. If it wasn't for her and that damn bet I wouldn't be in the situation that I was in. After everything that happened I still wanted that man. That shit was pissing me off, because I normally had better control of my feelings.

"You don't owe me an apology Devin. Your mental ass ex does. I don't think I want one from her though. She might try to finish the job. I'm not going to sit back and wait for her to do that. Obviously the no class having hoe still wants you and I won't stand in her way." With that said I put my dark shades back on and closed my eyes.

"So, you think I'm leavin' now?" He asked before sitting down on the towel beside me.

I sighed in fake annoyance. Damn, he smelled so damn good.

"I know that we really just met, but when I'm with you I just feel something that I ain't never felt wit' another woman." He cleared his throat. "I don't know how to do this. I mean, I don't know how to knowingly…share a woman and I know that the situation wit' Amil didn't make shit any easier for you. Damn." He let out a sigh. "I'm feelin' you Fanci. Everything about you. You ain't like the women I'm used to dealin' wit'. I know that I ain't nothing like the men you used to dealin' with either. That's probably a good thing because it's clear that our past relationships didn't work. I mean, you're still married…but anyway. What I'm sayin' is you don't have to be miserable wit' dude. Just know that I ain't a broke ass nigga. I got money. Maybe I can't give you the life that he gives you, but baby, I can give you a life."

What he was saying sounded good, but I already knew better. If he only knew that I wouldn't get any kind of support from my husband if we got a divorce. My mother depended on me to pay her massive bills. Maybe that was why Isaac and I had so many problems. Not only did he take care of me, but he took care of my mother too. If I left Isaac Devin wasn't going to be able to afford to take care of my mother too. Shit, that bitch Amil lived off him, so he'd be taking care of three women. That wouldn't work.

"You do not want to take on my baggage Devin. You barely know me, so you don't know the half. Not only that, but I damn sure don't want to take on yours." I stood up and glared down at him. "I don't even know why you came here. I'm so done with whatever you think we had. I enjoyed myself, but it was just a fling. I'm going back to my suite and I'm going to try to forget that this unwanted reunion ever happened. I hope you enjoy the rest of your time in Miami, but it won't be with me."

He wasn't budging from the towel, so I decided to walk off and let him have it. Before I could get to the beachfront property he was beside me with the towel in his hand.

"I know you didn't mean any of that and your emotions are talkin' right now. There has to be a reason why you're okay wit' bein' trapped in a relationship that is not fulfilling you. If you were bein' satisfied in every way our little fling, as you called it, would not have happened. In the small amount of time that you've known me you've probably felt more alive than you have since the day you said I do to that muthafucka. You know for a fact that I have done things to your body that you never thought were humanly possible. I know baby because I was there. I'm there ma. Shit, I'm bein' vulnerable and open and I ain't never done that. This aint' just physical Fanci. It's more and I want all of it. You know you feel the same way and after what we've shared you can't go back to feelin' unloved and not havin' that sexy ass body treated like it should be."

My skin instantly felt like it was on fire, and it wasn't the sun because it had already set to dusk. Why was he there? Why was he making shit so damn hard for me? Damnit he was making me feel things I didn't need to feel. I knew that feeling what I felt would put me right back where I didn't need to be; not able to maintain the lifestyle I wanted. Not only that, but he had a child by a buffoon. I wasn't trying to deal with that bitch on a daily, but damn, he was right. Being around him had given me life and the sex was bomb. Not only that, but we communicated so well, which was a rarity for me when it came to men. He seemed to like my brash nature and blunt way of talking.

"I'm not really trying to hear any more of this Devin." I stopped walking and faced him. "I can't do this with you. Both of us have complicated ass situations and I'm not trying to add any more drama to my already crazy life. It was fun while it lasted, but like I told you before, I'm done. The End. Curtain closed." I rubbed my hands together as if I was removing the dirt. "My hands are clean. Have a nice life."

When I turned to walk away he grabbed my arm and turned me around to face him. Before I could slap that fool, or respond to the sudden physical contact he leaned over and kissed me. It wasn't just a peck either, but a kiss that was filled with so much pent up passion and desire that my head almost burst. Damn him. I was caught up in the rapture. I couldn't fight that shit, even if I wanted to and for some reason...I didn't want to.

Chapter 8

Fanci

Of course I experienced the best sex of my life in Miami with Devin. As hard as I'd tried to act he'd shattered my glass wall in no time. It was just too damn easy for him and it made me feel so weak. I was all in my feelings, but I tried to make the best of our time there. Shit, at least Amil couldn't just pop up and shoot at me again.

We were back in Georgia, so the subject of Amil shooting at me came up. I knew that pressing charges against her would only expose our affair, but I needed to know that he had laid down the law. She had to know that there were consequences if she ever tried some shit like that again.

"I talked to her and she claims she didn't shoot at you. Now we both know that's bullshit, but she threatened to turn me in for giving her the gun and having guns if I tried to report her."

I understood how that threat didn't stand too well with him being that he was on parole. Devin didn't hide anything about himself. As much as it put a bad taste in my mouth, I also knew how hard it was to have a different mentality growing up where we did. In my case I had a mother around that cared and that was a rarity where we came from.

"Damn, so she wants to play hard ball huh? I guess we are going to have to find another way to be together, because your place is no longer an option." I knew that going to hotels in the city wouldn't be a good idea, but not being with Devin was not an option either. We had to come up with something.

"I agree, so when will I see you again so I can get to work planning something nice and romantic."

Damn, I loved the way he talked. Not only was his voice nice to listen to, but his way of talking was refreshing. It was nice not to always hear that condescending "I'm so educated," bullshit that Issac spat all day with his drunk ass.

"It'll have to be next week. Isaac's daughter is graduating from high school on Friday. I'm not looking forward to it though. She hates me, which is probably because her bitter mother and her old fart of a grandmother raised her to. I can't stand Isaac's family. They don't think I'm good enough for him."

Devin didn't say anything for a while and I thought he'd hung up.

"Hello?"

"I'm here. I was just counting the days. Damn, four days seem like forever baby."

I laughed. "That's nothing. Think about all of the years that you didn't know me. You survived didn't you?"

"Nah, I don't wanna think about that, but you're right. I guess I'll make it."

I heard the sound of the alarm alerting that the front door had been opened.

"I'm gonna call you back," I said quickly and hung up without waiting for his response.

Besides, Devin knew the protocol. If I abruptly hung up he was aware that Isaac must've made his grand entrance.

Isaac walked into the room without even saying a mere hello to me. I didn't get a kiss or any kind of look of interest. He was back to his old cold ways and that was fine by me. It wasn't like I wanted anything more from him. As long as I was married to him it would afford me material things, not love. I was aware of that and used to it at that point. Devin filled the void and that was fine by me.

Suddenly he looked up from his cell phone after putting his brief case down on the floor.

"Did you get your dress for Megan's graduation yet?" There was a frown on his face and I knew that he was ready for his after work drink.

"Yes, I've had it for weeks now. I tried it on for you." I shook my head. That man was the worst.

He had a thoughtful look on his face like he was trying to remember. When he walked off I was sure that he didn't, so it was time for him to pour a glass of sin. His drink of choice was vodka. Most of the time he'd drink Grey Goose with no chaser until he passed out.

At first he didn't drink so much, but I think his mother often pressured him to go back to Med School. He had settled for being a professor after feeling like he was a failure when it came to becoming a doctor. Of course he was under pressure to walk in his mother and father's footsteps, but he just didn't make the cut. He had been terminated from the medical program at Morehouse, so he decided to teach Biology on the collegiate level instead.

Iris constantly reminded him that he was a failure to his family's legacy. I guess constantly hearing that he wasn't anything like she wanted him to be had to hurt. She often blamed it on him being married to me, but he was a professor when I met him. She should've blamed his first damn wife for that shit.

He returned to the room with a tumbler full of warm vodka. He didn't even bother to add ice. I turned up my nose and shook my head at him. That shit was so damn sad. He needed to go to rehab and attend AA meetings, but everybody around him turned a blind eye to his drinking.

On the other hand I had my own issues. I'd often gone through bouts of depression throughout my life that were sometimes very severe. I'd been prescribed several anti-depressants, but I hated the way they made me feel all loopy. I would rather be alert and able to feel. It wasn't like every day was going to be perfect and I wasn't going to keep expecting that. I knew for a fact that nobody's life was full of sunny days. Sometimes there were storms that would come and rock your world. My marriage to Isaac and my situation with Devin were two of them.

"Well, I need to see the dress again. Go put it on," he said in a bossy tone.

I hated when he tried to order me around. That shit made me want to cut his ass. One pet peeve about him that I had was when he tried to control what I wore. He had to approve of my outfits like I didn't know how to dress myself. That was some downgrading shit. It made me feel like he didn't think I was capable of looking like a lady or something.

"I can't help it if you don't remember me trying it on before. I'm not trying it on again. I have somewhere to go." I jumped up from the sofa and walked toward the stairs.

Honestly, I didn't have anywhere to go. I just needed to get the hell away from him before I did something permanent to his ass. I knew the combination to the safe that held his beloved Colt 45 Pistol that his father had once owned. If prison didn't scare the fuck out of me I'd use that gun to put him out of his misery, thus saving me from mine.

* * *

As I pulled up in Janai's driveway I noticed that there was some drama going on with the neighbors across the street from her. Being that I hadn't called to let her know that I was popping up, I had no clue what was going on. All I knew was I saw some chick throwing clothes out on the front lawn. The dude who they must've belonged to was running out of the door frantically trying to stop her.

I couldn't hear him, but I was sure he was pleading his case.

When I saw the chick squirt lighter fluid on the pile of clothes I knew that shit was about to get real. Dude was yelling, but I couldn't make out what he was saying because I had my windows up. I turned my car off and literally walked backwards to Janai's front door. While I waited I kept my eyes on the scene that was unfolding. Next thing I knew, old girl dropped a match and his clothes were engulfed in flames.

Uh oh, dude was pissed. His hands were on old girl's shoulders and he was shaking the shit out of her.

"I told you I don't want her Kristie! Why the hell you doing this shit. Our fucking kids are in the house!" He yelled.

Damn, everybody was cheating. Was anybody actually happy in their relationship?

She screamed back, "Your kids need to know that you ain't shit! I ain't hiding nothing from them. Their daddy is a fucking whore. You wasn't thinking about them when you had that home wrecking bitch in my house! You better get the fuck away from me before I set your black, sorry ass on fire!"

"C'mon bitch," Janai said behind me. "Let's watch inside."

I was so engulfed in what was going on across the street that I didn't even hear her open the door. We scurried in the house and peeked through the blinds like two nosey old women.

"Damn," Janai hissed when Kristie started squirting lighter fluid on him.

Suddenly he backed up and I laughed. "He better not get too close to that damn fire or that's going to be his ass."

"Shit, they fight all the time. Instead of calling the cops we just watch. She caught him fucking some chick in their bed when she was supposed to be at the movies with the kids."

I looked at her. "How you know that?"

"Oh, I was outside at the mailbox when the shit first popped off. She was obviously setting his ass up because she was only gone for an hour. I guess he planned to fuck his mistress and send her away before wifee got back. Ha. She had something for that ass. You should've seen that hoe getting up out of there. She had a huge ass butcher knife after her. This shit's been going on for a while now."

I shook my head as I watched dude run toward a red Dodge Charger. He wasn't trying to get burned like those clothes. Obviously he didn't have his belt on because his pants suddenly started to fall down and so did he, right on his face.

As I howled in uncontrollable laughter Janai fell down to her knees in tears. He got up real quick and held his pants up. When he opened the car door, he threw one last look over his shoulder to see if she was behind him. He got the hell up out there and Kristie sprayed the blazing inferno with the water hose before stumping off into the house.

"Well damn," I said when I was finally able to stop laughing.

"Whew girl, that was hilarious," Janai said as she stood up.

"Yes, I damn sure needed that laugh. Just glad I didn't witness a murder. That would've just been too much for the day."

"Hmm, so what's wrong bestie? You might as well go ahead and spill it. You didn't make a pop up visit on me for nothing. You better be glad I ain't have my boo thang over here. You would've been standing right out there watching them brawl while I was enjoying a brawl of my own." She winked at me and we shared a laugh.

"Well, where do I start? Isaac..."

"Hold that thought," she said suddenly before sprinting out of the room.

When she came back she had a small plastic baggie in her hand and some joint papers.

"Now, carry on."

* * *

At Megan's graduation party I stayed to myself and texted Devin the entire time. The graduation seemed to last forever and there we were at Isaac's ex-wife Lorraine's house. I did not want to be there at all. Honestly I could give two shits about his spoiled brat of a daughter graduating. As I took a drink of champagne I secretly wished she'd get pregnant her first year of college and show daddy and everybody else that she wasn't perfect either.

Like always nobody was talking to me and I couldn't care less about that either. All I wanted to do was get the fuck out of there. Damn, I should've driven my car. Isaac didn't even bother to mention the damn graduation party. Asshole. He already knew that I wouldn't have wanted to come.

After draining my glass I wandered into the kitchen and caught Iris and Lorraine in the midst of a conversation about me. I stood by the door, so they wouldn't see me. It was the perfect spot because from where they were standing I was out of their view.

"Did you see that tattoo on her leg? I told you she was from the ghetto and she looks like a cheap whore," Lorraine spat with venom.

"I don't know what my stupid son was thinking. I always wanted him with you and…"

"Fuck both of you jealous ass bitches!" I was sick of them and it was time that they both knew how I really felt.

I'd had too much to drink, so it was like my anger had finally boiled over. I didn't give a damn about the fact that it was Megan's party. What better place for a confrontation that should've happened years ago.

"Don't ruin my daughter's party! I'll get your trifling ass escorted out of here!" Lorraine shot back.

"I'm ruining her party? Bitch bye! I hope her life gets ruined just like yours. I hope a gang banger knocks her up and leaves her to raise the child by herself. Nobody wants you. You're alone and I have your ex-husband. Are you mad

Lorraine?" I flashed a fake smile her way and she lunged toward me.

I had the champagne glass in my hand and as we tussled it dropped and broke. After kicking her in the gut she finally let me go and Iris's old ass was yelling all frantic like I was the one who had jumped on Lorraine. When I looked down at the floor I noticed that the handle of the glass was sharp, so I picked it up to use as a weapon.

Lorraine got up and walked toward me again.

"I'll cut you bitch. You better back up." I held the glass out at her, but she still was coming closer. That bitch was asking for me to cut her ass.

There was too much pent up anger inside of me and I was tired of taking bullshit. I'd been taking it for too long and at that moment I didn't really care. I didn't want to cut Lorraine, but she'd better not move anther damn inch.

"Put the glass down Fanci," I heard Isaac's voice behind me.

"Tell her to back up off me then. She jumped on me. That's why the champagne glass broke. She could've cut me," I said keeping my eye on Lorraine's crazy ass.

What the hell? First I get shot at and now that shit.

"Are you okay Fanci?" He asked.

I could tell that he was sober, so he seemed to have some compassion toward me for once.

"That heifer is trying to ruin our daughter's party," Lorraine spoke up trying to defend her jealous actions.

"Yes, she stormed in here ready to fight like the ghetto bitch that she is. You should've seen…" Iris started to lie and I cut her off.

"Tell the truth. I walked in here to get another drink and you two were standing there talking about me. You said Isaac is stupid and you always wanted him to be with her old, ugly ass."

"That is not true," Iris said with her eyes casted down.

Lying old hag. I hated her with a passion.

"It is true! You were talking about my tattoo and how ghetto I am Lorraine! Then when I said that you were jealous you jumped on me. Tell the truth you wrinkled, dried up…"

"You got a tattoo?" Isaac asked with wide eyes.

"Is that really important right now?" I asked shaking my head.

Suddenly Megan walked into the kitchen. I was sure that nobody had heard the commotion over the music, but she could probably tell that the situation was volatile. At the sight of a sharp piece of glass in my hand and her mother breathing all hard, she knew that there had been a fight. It was obvious.

"I hate her daddy! Why did you marry her? She ruins everything!" She shrieked and stormed out of the room.

My head was swimming and I wanted to go off and really hurt somebody, but I didn't. Instead I dropped the piece of glass.

"Take me home Isaac! Now!"

* * *

"Dayum, the hood came out of your ass bitch! Shit, I wish I was there. Somebody would've got fucked up. Even that lil' bitch Megan with her spoiled rotten ass," Janai cackled as we talked on the phone later that night.

"Right. I knew it was in there somewhere."

She cleared her throat. "Well, I was calling you because I went over your prenup with my lawyer friend and like I said, there is a loophole."

I was interested. "Okay, tell me more." I needed an out and fast.

When we were in the car Isaac had gone off on me because of the tattoo, but not because of what had just happened. In his eyes it was ghetto to get a tattoo and honestly that was probably the reason that I didn't get one before the bet. I pointed out to him that he hadn't even noticed it himself and he was my husband. That bitch Lorraine was looking at me a little too damn hard and he wasn't looking at me hard enough. That wasn't my damn problem.

"Well, it says that in the event that you can prove infidelity on his part and divorce is a result, you will be granted alimony, and half of his assets as well as seventy five percent of your business. The pot would be even sweeter if ya'll had a child," she explained.

"Hmm, if he's cheating on me that would explain why he's so cold. I don't know though. He's always here and…"

Janai cut me off. "Maybe she's a student and it's going on at his job."

"That would make sense Nai." I thought about it. What if he had traded me in for a younger woman?

"Well, either we hire a private investigator or we play detectives. Honestly, spying on him may be fun. We can go up to the college and maybe I'll find a young ass nigga to do me like Devin's been doing you." She broke out in laughter and I shook my head.

"You're a mess Nai. I could hire a PI, but I don't know about that yet. Maybe I can just do a little snooping myself first and if I don't find anything we'll take that route." It was crazy that I was actually hoping that my husband was cheating on me.

Shit, getting pregnant by him was definitely not going to happen.

* * *

"I'm so sorry baby, but Isaac provides for you. Him cheating is a small thing. At least he doesn't hit you or…"

I tuned my mother out because it was the same conversation every time we talked. It was easy for her to say that because if it wasn't for him she wouldn't have that beautiful house in Stone Mountain. When I thought about it, it was like she was pimping me out. Was that her agenda in the first place? Was that why she was so hell bent on me marrying a man who was well off?

"Mom, hitting a woman is not the only form of abuse. He neglects me and he's mentally abusive. I don't expect for you to understand. As long as your bills are paid and you can go to Bingo on Tuesdays you don't give a damn about what I'm going through." I shook my head knowing that it would be best for us to just get off the phone.

"I'm your mother Fanci and I gave you everything you ever asked for when you was a child. I can't believe that you're talking to me this way!"

I was livid at that point. "It's like you're making me feel like I owe you for that. I'm your daughter and you were supposed to take care of me."

She sighed. "What's going on with you? Are you pregnant?"

"No, I'm not pregnant ma," I huffed. "Look, I'm in traffic right now. I'll call you back." Before she could say anything else I ended the call.

I was on my way to do some shopping before I headed to the office. There was no point in all work and no play. I had to find some sexy lingerie to wear for Devin. The plan was for us to head to Savannah later that night. It was only a four hour drive, so if we left at six we'd get to our hotel at around ten. It was perfect and Isaac thought I was at a convention to sell toys. Ha, if only he knew. It was my time to have fun before my investigative work began.

* * *

BANG! BANG! BANG!

"Open up, it's the police!"

"What the?" Devin whispered and jumped up to put on his boxers.

We'd been making the maddest, most passionate love in our hotel suite in Savannah before being rudely interrupted.

"The police?" I asked.

Shit, what had happened to regular security?

I scrambled to get dressed as Devin moved toward the suite's door.

"I'll be back babe. Let me clear this up," he said before closing the bedroom door behind him.

I sighed as my heart pounded against my rib cage. It was like I could hear it. My adrenaline was already pumping after several orgasms. I knew that we were loud, but were we that damn loud?

Chapter 9

Devin

When I opened the door I was face to face with two, white uniformed police officers. That shit was just my luck being that I was on parole. With the way black men were being killed by the cops lately, I tried my best to play it cool.

"Uh, can I help you?" I asked looking from one of them to the other.

The shorter one with the blonde hair spoke up first.

"We got a call that there was a domestic disturbance here. Is there somebody else here? There was a report of a female screaming for her life."

I almost laughed. Fanci *was* pretty loud, but whoever had called the cops was exaggerating. Either that or the cops were stretching the truth.

"There is a female here, but her life has not been threatened in any way," I tried to assure them.

The taller, older, more tanned officer stepped forward. "I'm Officer Rollins and this is Officer Oliver. Well, we'd like to come inside to make sure that she's okay."

I nodded. "Yes. Uh, c'mon in."

They stepped inside of the suite and the door slammed shut loudly behind them.

Without my instruction or inclusion they rushed off to find Fanci. When they finally did she assured them that we were simply making love.

"We're newlyweds and maybe we were a little loud. Why didn't security come first?" Fanci asked.

That was a believable explanation being that lots of couples honeymooned or even eloped in Savannah. I was glad that she had taken control of the situation. Her sophisticated nature made it so that the officers seemed to believe her.

"Yeah, this is our wedding night, so you know..." I added for good measure.

"Security made several attempts to knock at the door, but obviously you didn't hear them," Officer Rollins said with a frown on his face.

Officer Oliver grinned knowingly. "I got married a few months ago, so I know how it is. Just let us see some ID and we'll be on our way. Clearly neither of you have any physical signs of a fight."

My heart thumped in my chest. They were going to find out that I was on parole if they did a check on us. Fuck! Not only that, but what if for some reason that shit made it online somehow. Sometimes when people got citations for crazy shit their names and stories would appear on the internet. If we were arrested for a disturbance, or if they really thought I had assaulted Fanci, it would be public knowledge anyway.

I reached for my wallet that was in the pocket of my jeans that I'd put on right before I opened the door.

The sound of a strange female's voice filled the room. It was their walkie talkies. I didn't recognize the number code or understand what she was saying, but Officer Rollins responded.

"In route."

He glared at me. "Keep it down. If we get another call we're hauling you both in."

Officer Oliver nodded in agreement, but he had an amused look on his face. "And congratulations."

"Thank you," Fanci gushed.

When they left we both let out sighs of relief before laughing.

"That was close as hell," she said with a smile.

"But it was worth every second that I was inside of your sweetness." If only it was true. I wished that we were newlyweds.

She kissed me deeply. "Umm, well, since they're gone how about round three."

I stared her down and licked my lips. "You sure? You know I'm on parole and shit. You gotta try to hold it together."

"Well, why don't you gag me?" She winked and I was on hard in an instant.

"Damn." I shook my head in disbelief. That woman never ceased to amaze me and that was why I couldn't get enough of her fine ass.

*   *   *

"I need to stop at my crib and make sure that Biggie and Tupac are good," I explained to Fanci when we made it back.

Biggie and Tupac were my pit bulls. They were house dogs, but when Fanci came around I put them in the basement. She was afraid of dogs and I respected that being that pits got a bad rep.

She let out a sigh. "Can you just take me to my car first?"

She had parked at Janai's which was about an hour from my crib. I got to my spot first and so I thought it was best to do a quick stop.

"I mean, if you want," I said wondering why she was acting all funny. We'd had a good time in Savannah. Well, other than the police showing up.

"I don't want to run into Amil's cray ass."

Oh, so that's what it was.

"It's nine in the morning Fanci. I doubt that lazy ass woman is up." Shit, when we were together she didn't get up until noon.

"Okay, stop at your place and check on your dogs. If something happens to them in the hour that it takes to get to Janai's I'd feel so guilty. Plus, I'm hungry too. I want some breakfast."

"Where you want to eat at? If you want breakfast we can go to J Christopher's. It's one on the way to Janai's crib," I said feeling hungry myself.

She nodded. "That'll work."

* * *

We were seated at a booth waiting for the server to bring us our coffee. The J. Christopher's in downtown Decatur on Ponce De Leon was the type of spot that was mostly patronized by white people. It was a restaurant located in the downtown area that only sold breakfast and brunch. The hours were from 7 am until 2 pm.

I figured that it was low key enough for us not to run into anybody that we knew. Besides, Fanci lived all the way in Alpharetta and her in laws did too. She didn't have to worry about them venturing to Decatur. Well, at least we hoped not.

"Oh my fucking God," Fanci gasped as she rolled her eyes. "I knew you should've taken me to my car."

"Why? What's wrong?" I asked.

"Your psychotic ass baby mama's here."

I looked back and there Amil was sitting down at the booth behind us. Well, she was behind me.

"Damnit," I said under my breath and shook my head.

Our server came back and placed a red, coffee pot in front of us with mugs to match. "Your food will be right out," she said with a gleeful smile.

Our expressions didn't match hers. I was sitting across from Fanci, so she was face to face with Amil's cray cray ass.

"I can't believe her," Fanci said as I poured some coffee in my mug.

I sighed. "Me either. I'm 'bout to talk to her. I'm not gonna let her ruin…"

"Save it Devin. I've already lost my appetite."

My heart sank. Why the hell was Amil so stuck on me? She'd said that she was going to make my life a living hell if I wasn't with her. I guess she meant that shit for real. At first I doubted that it would be so bad, but I was wrong as hell.

I shook my head and got up. When I sat beside Amil she had a huge ass smile on her face. I glanced at Fanci and noticed the tense look on hers. All I needed her to do was hold it together until I got rid of my ex.

"What the hell? C'mon Amil. This is crazy as hell and once again where the hell is my child?" I was pissed the fuck off.

"Londyn's fine, but I'm not. I told you not to keep tryna play me Devin." Amil took a breath and then closed her eyes as if she was attempting to keep her temper in check.

She'd always had a bad temper and I always chucked it up to her fucked up ass childhood. She'd been through so much and so had I. In my attempt at finding love and trying to comfort her, I ignored a lot of bad signs. Amil had always tried to fight or harm women that she thought were connected to me, but I thought she'd change eventually.

"I ain't tryna play you." I shook my head. "We've been over for a long time. Why do you keep fooling yourself woman? How'd you know that I was here?"

"I followed you," she said simply.

"You followed me? Why the fuck would you do that? C'mon Amil. The shit you're doing is crazy for real. If I report your ass for this shit I'm sure I could get my child. Now where the hell is she?"

"I noticed that you hadn't been home for a few days, so I parked a few houses down and waited to see if you'd be back today. When I saw you had that bitch in the car I followed ya'll. Londyn's fine, don't worry. She's all you fuckin' care about." She rolled her eyes and pretended to look at the menu.

"Londyn is all I have left now that my parents are dead and you know that. My only sister lives in DC and we ain't that close. I know you tryna get to me and shit, but I don't know why. You act like I don't take care of mine."

"I was supposed to be yours Devin, but you threw me away. How do I know that you won't do the same shit to Londyn? You might feel like you love her now, but you claimed to love me too…"

"It's not the same."

"Hmm. You better be glad I ain't been able to catch that bitch alone." She was still pretending to be looking over the menu.

"So, like I thought, you shot at her."

She shrugged her shoulders indifferently. "I ain't shoot at that hoe. If I had she wouldn't be sitting there. She'd be dead as hell. I just shot in the air. I thought it would scare the hoe away, but I see that it didn't."

I was so frustrated with her. We were in a public place so it wasn't much that I could do. There was no way that I was about to act a fool and go ham in front of all of those white folks. My parole was almost over and so I wasn't taking any chances.

"Leave Amil. You know that what you're doing is uncalled for." I shook my head. "Just go home."

There was a look of a pure evil in her eyes as she stared at me. "Fuck you and that bitch!"

She said it loud enough for Fanci to hear her. Before I could stop her Fanci was standing there at the table.

"Nah bitch, fuck you!" She spat venomously before throwing a cold cup of iced water in Amil's face.

"Ah shit." I grabbed Fanci and quickly led her toward the exit.

I could hear Amil screaming out threats behind us and then I felt her trying to pull me away from Fanci.

"Let me go Amil!" I yelled having to let Fanci go so that I could grab Amil.

All that did was give Fanci the opportunity to punch the shit out of her.

"Shit, stop Fanci." I turned around and tried to shield Amil from the assault. "Go to the car."

"Fuck that! That bitch tried to kill me!" Fanci lunged and tried to land another punch over my shoulder, but I wouldn't let her.

Next thing I knew some chick was walking over and I figured that she was part of management.

"You're going to have to leave or we're calling the police," she explained nervously.

At the mention of the police being called Fanci took a deep breath and walked off. Once she was in the car I turned to Amil.

"I don't know what makes you think I'll ever be wit' you, especially after this." I shook my head and walked off.

"Whatever nigga. I got this," Amil stated calmly.

To my surprise she didn't attempt to stop me. As I got in my car behind the wheel I noticed that she was staring me down with hatred in her eyes. I knew that she had something up her sleeve, but I didn't know what. My plan was to keep it together and watch my back as well as Fanci's. Damn, I had to get Londyn away from her crazy ass asap.

Chapter 10

Fanci

I was back home trying to forget about the scene with Amil. That psycho bitch had actually followed us and planted her ass in a booth right next to us. The nerve of her. I'd tried my hardest not to react, but how much could a bitch take? She was trying me and I knew that I could put my hands on her without getting shot up. There was no way she'd go there in a restaurant full of witnesses.

"See, that's why I didn't want to stop at your place first. That stalker of yours was waiting for us." I shook my head as I slowly undressed and sat down at my vanity.

That heifer better be glad I didn't decide to throw some hot coffee in her face.

"I know and once again I'm sorry," Devin said with a sigh. "I hope this doesn't mean you want to give up on me again. We'll just have to stay away from my place baby. I promise things won't always be like this. Just be patient with me like I am with you."

I was taken aback. "You're being patient with me? What the fuck does that mean? My husband isn't the problem in our relationship, your ex bitch is." The audacity of his ass. Patient with me? Get the fuck outta here.

He sighed. "That's not what I meant."

"Well, what the fuck did you mean?" I removed my earrings and brushed my hair up into a ponytail.

"Nothing. Let's just talk later. It's been a crazy day and I know that you just wanna relax 'cause I damn sure do."

Hmm, so he was going to shut down. It was cool. I needed a nap anyway. I was exhausted and I needed some chill time before starting my quest to find out if Isaac had been cheating. Being that I was an attractive woman, that had to be the only explanation. At one point he couldn't keep his hands off me and suddenly it was like the sight of me repulsed him. Something had to give and soon.

"Okay," I agreed. "Guess I'll call you later."

"A'ight. Later then," he said and hung up.

I hung up and slid on a comfortable pair of gray cotton shorts and tank top to match. Isaac wasn't home and I was grateful. All I needed was a short power nap before I went online and checked out who he had been calling on his cell phone. We were on a family plan so I had access to all of the phone numbers he dialed. My plan was to find out if he had been unfaithful so that I could get out of my miserable marriage with what I deserved.

* * *

"Shit, I know I tried for you and Devin at first, but that bitch Amil is out of hand. I don't know Fanc," Janai said as she helped me snoop around the house to see if I could find anything.

I had the money to hire a private investigator, but I really didn't want anybody else in my business. I'd printed out months of phone records and highlighted numbers that stood out. Those numbers were ones that I didn't recognize. I had Iris, Lorraine and Megan's numbers in my phone. Anybody else that he was conversing with made me suspicious. I wasn't jealous in anyway at all. I was just desperate to get a divorce and be able to take care of myself.

"I'm not worried about Amil. It's been two weeks and she's been unusually quiet. Devin said she's even been cooperative about him getting Londyn. I saw pictures of her. She's so cute. Makes me want to make a baby with him. I'm sure our baby would be even cuter being that I look a thousand times better than Amil's hood rat ass." I rolled my eyes at the thought of her.

Janai sighed. "Okay, but it's your life not mine. If you ever need me to help take care of that hoe just let me know. You know I got you."

I smiled. "I know boo, now let's get back to it. Our goal is to find some evidence of Isaac cheating. Devin's situation is obsolete right now."

"You're right." She took a breath, closed her eyes and massaged her temples. "I have to focus."

Unlike me, Janai was a master snooper. She had always been the one who knew how to find the dirt on her men. I wasn't one to go around looking for shit. Honestly, I just didn't know how.

"Did you call the numbers you found?" Janai asked curiously as I stared at the itemized list with random highlights of yellow, pink and light blue.

"Yeah, but I only got automated voicemails with no names. I'm still at square one. I'm stuck." I groaned and sat down in the computer chair.

Janai rubbed my back supportively. "You're not stuck. Just be patient."

I sighed. "You sound like Devin."

"I know that I'm back and forth with this. At first I was against it and then I saw how happy you were. Now I'm back to not feeling good about your situation with Devin. I think I let your happiness blind me and you are too. Don't be a fool for either of them boo. Just leave Isaac and be single for a while. That'll be best for you."

Be single? I didn't know how to do that. I'd always had a man. Shit, I wasn't trying to grow old alone and end up like my mother. Hell no. That was no life at all. That was not an option, but I didn't want my best friend to judge me. She was so much more independent than me and didn't need a man's presence to feel complete. If only I was more like her. I didn't like for my bed to be empty at night, so I had to make sure that everything worked in my favor.

"I'm not like you Nai. I don't like being single." I sighed and tears stung my eyes. "I just want to get this over with so I can be with Devin and have everything that Isaac owes me. I didn't go through all of this shit for nothing."

"It's not that I like being single Fanci. I just like being happy. It doesn't matter if I'm single or not. I don't let a man validate me and my happiness. If I am fortunate enough to have a good man in my life one day that'll be great. I'm not anti-love. I just won't settle for bullshit for the sake of not being alone. I can't. That's just not me. I'm not judging you, but in order for you to be happy with somebody else you have to be happy with you. If you can't stand being alone with yourself who's going to want to be around you? You have to love yourself bestie and then everything else will fall into place."

"Okay Iyanla," I laughed.

She rolled her eyes. "See, I can't with you bitch. You're so childish." There was a smile on her face that let me know that she was just as amused as I was by my comment.

"Oh, stop being so damn sensitive woman," I said and playfully shoved her.

"I'm for real though Fanci. You let Miss Clarine brain wash you into believing that you're nothing without a man, but that's not true."

I didn't really want to hear her motivational speech, so I cut that shit short. "Can you just help me please?"

She sighed and looked around Isaac's office. "Okay, I don't think anything will be in here. Does he have a safe or something?"

"Yeah, but I know the combination. He'd be stupid to hide anything in there," I protested.

"Not really. Sometimes men hide stuff in obvious places because they know you won't expect for them to hide them there." She shook her head like I was so naïve and didn't know shit.

"Yeah, there is a safe in the master bedroom's closet. It's built into the wall."

"Okay, show me where it is."

I led her to our bedroom and opened the closet door. Once I found the safe, I opened it and stood back for her to look through it. She went through piles of papers and then bypassed the cash to grab a small, black case. It was the case that held his gun.

"Oh, that's his gun his father left him," I said knowing that it was nothing else in there.

Janai gave me a look and opened the case anyway. She used her t shirt to pick up the gun and there a business card was.

"Tamia Jones, no job title, just a phone number," she said thoughtfully.

I grabbed the card and studied it. It was plain and white with black writing. "Why would he put that in there?"

"Because prissy little Fanci would not look in his gun case. Compare that number to the numbers you found."

That was a smart idea, so I jumped up to do just that. There it was highlighted in pink several times over.

"Hmmm, sorry ass bastard," I hissed under my breath although I was being unfaithful too. In my case I felt that it was warranted being that he didn't give me one ounce of love or affection. He never even told me that he loved me anymore, so why would I expect for him to show it?

I was kind of upset, but relieved at the same time. I finally had the evidence that I needed.

"Now we just have to catch him in the act," Janai said with a thoughtful look on her face.

* * *

Devin

Damn, I couldn't believe how calm and cooperative Amil was being. It was kind of scary because it made me think that maybe she was up to something. When I called her out on it she laughed it off and said that she'd overreacted.

"You were right. I thought about what I was doing. It wasn't called for at all. I was just caught up in my emotions and now I'm thinking about our daughter. If I do some dumb shit she'll end up without me and I'm her mother. Killing some hoe that you're fuckin' just ain't worth me being separated from her. Shit, I know how that feels." Her eyes filled with tears, but I didn't know if I should believe her or not.

"Are you for real Amil? Are you finally ready to act like a real mother?" My eyes bore into hers.

"Yes." She didn't look away. "I am. Londyn's in daycare right now, but I let them know that you'll be picking her up. Just don't have my child around her. This is your time."

I nodded. "You don't have to worry about that. It's just gonna be me and my baby girl the entire weekend."

"Good." There was a smile on her face.

I shook my head. "This is too good to be true."

"No it's not. I know now that what's meant to be will be." Amil walked to the door and left without saying anything else. She hadn't even brought up the fight with Fanci at J.Christopher's. Was she finally over it? I hoped so.

I just shook my head and managed to smile. Now that things were falling into place with Amil I was hoping to finally get my woman. I wanted Fanci all to myself to live happily ever after with. It was just a matter of convincing her to leave her husband. I loved my daughter, but in my heart I was hoping that one day she'd give me the son I always wanted.

*   *   *

"I'm about to drop Londyn off and then head back to the crib. I hope we can spend some time together," I told Fanci.

"Well, Janai has a nice spot on Lake Allatoona. I got the key," she said in a sexy voice. "At least your baby mama don't know about it and we won't have to worry about police because there are no neighbors close by. Let's not ride together. I'll meet you there."

"I'm there baby. What time?"

"Meet me there at around eight o' clock tonight."

"Sounds like a plan ma. See you then beautiful."

"Okay."

I hung up with a huge smile on my face. As I glanced over at my daughter I couldn't help but think that I'd finally be able to get full custody of her. She'd have the mother that she deserved when I ended up with Fanci. Deep down inside I didn't believe that bullshit Amil was spitting.

* * *

We were both breathing hard and twisted up in the sheets after a passionate session. My fingers grazed her skin as she laid lazily in my arms.

"Wow, that was…"

"Amazing like always," she finished for me.

I chuckled and kissed her cheek. Her hair was a little wavy from the humidity and sweat of our bedroom rump. Damn, that shit was so sexy. There was no makeup on her face and she was naked and all natural. I loved it.

"You look amazing. You're so beautiful Fanci," I said breathlessly.

It was like I was obsessed with her or something, because she was always on my mind. Not being able to be with her when and how I wanted to was making me crazy. I had to let her know how I really felt.

"Thank you with your sexy self," she said before kissing my chest.

She moved down to my belly button and then peered up at me with wide eyes. "He's awake."

"What is this gonna end up being Fanci?" I asked feeling as if I sounded like a bitch.

I *was* hard, but being in a relationship with her was on my mind, not sex.

She sighed and then moved to lean against the pillow. "I don't know Devin. I'm working on it."

"What do you mean you're working on it? Just file for a divorce," I protested. "It's not like ya'll have kids and shit. What the fuck…"

"We have investments. You wouldn't understand…"

"Oh, so this is about money. What, ya'll got a prenup or something?"

She was silent and when I looked down at her there were tears in her eyes.

"It's complicated okay. We're not here to talk about that. We were having a great time and…"

"I'm sorry baby," I sighed. "I'm just frustrated. I don't want you with him anymore. The thought of him sleeping in the same bed with you makes me wanna…"

I closed my eyes. "I don't even wanna think about that shit. It burns me up Fanci. That shit's crazy because I know that you were married to that nigga before you met me, but I'm ready for you to just end that shit and be wit' me. I love you."

She looked up at me in surprise and the tears really started falling. "I love you too Devin."

It was the first time either of us had said those words and I knew that shit was real. I was falling for Fanci so hard and I knew that I wanted her to be my wife one day. In order for that to happen she had to leave her husband. My patience was wearing thin. She would have to make a choice eventually because what we had was deeper than we'd ever planned it would be.

"Fling my ass then," I said when we finally broke our kiss.

She nodded in agreement. "This was never a fling."

I kissed her sexy lips again. "I knew yo' ass was just talking."

She giggled. "I'm hungry."

"Me too. How about I grill us some T-Bones and potatoes with toss salad?"

"I know you are not asking me. Get your ass on up. I said I'm hungry." She pouted sexily.

I couldn't help but laugh. My baby was spoiled, but that was okay. She looked so cute when she was pretending to be pissed. As I leaned over and kissed her again I wondered if she would ever be mine. The thing was, I was willing to do just about anything to make that shit official.

Chapter 11

Fanci

After all of the snooping I'd done, it was about to pay off. I'd finally be free of Isaac and able to live the life that I wanted to live. Although I could see the light at the end of the tunnel, I was frazzled and had been suffering from anxiety attacks lately. I did have a panic disorder that had stemmed from feelings of inadequacy that was a result of me being an overachiever as a child. For some reason I never felt good enough and so I often tried too hard.

After visiting my doctor I was prescribed more Xanax and an anti-depressant that I couldn't remember the name of. I decided to pop a Xanax and drink a glass of Chardonnay before Janai and I ventured to the college to follow Isaac. There were two phone numbers that seemed to be consistent on the list. One belonged to the chick whose card we had found and the other belonged to some nameless bitch.

I'd attempted to call them both and I assumed that they were both screening their calls. Then on like the tenth attempt there was an answer for the number that we'd found in Isaac's gun case. Some chick answered talking about I had to set up an appointment and she was Tamia's assistant. Was Tamia Jones a call girl or something? Shit, at that point I was like fuck it. I'd just follow his ass and find out for myself. It was either Tamia the hoe or the other bitch.

"You ready?" Janai asked as we buckled our seatbelts.

I sighed. "Yeah."

She was driving her brother's black Nissan Sentra with dark tinted windows, which I hoped wasn't hot. We didn't have time to be getting pulled over by the cops. Reggie was still involved in the streets too, so his car reflected that. I was just glad that the car wouldn't be recognized by Isaac and he wouldn't be able to see who was inside. All I could do was hope for the best.

"You okay?" Janai asked as she peered over at me curiously.

"Not really." I sighed. "Devin's putting the pressure on me to leave Isaac. He's tired of waiting. He told me that he loves me."

"Wow, did you say it back?"

"Yeah, because I think I do."

"You think? Oh boy, and the shit gets deeper." Janai shook her head. "I feel sorry for you Fanc. I know you didn't plan any of this. Regardless of Devin, you need to leave Isaac. It shouldn't be the pressure that he's putting on you that's making you do this. Don't you want to be free of him whether you end up with Devin or not?"

"Yes, but it's hard to imagine my life without a man. What if Devin's not who I think he is? What if I just think it is love because I've gone without anything close to it from a man for so long? I don't know if it's just the good sex talking or what." I shook my head because I was so confused about how I felt.

"See, that's why you need to take some time to be single. You're rushing from one relationship to the other without taking the time for a breather. I know that you're enjoying him, but isn't he getting a little too serious. Maybe you shouldn't have told him you love him too. That would've been a hint for him to slow down."

I thought about it. "I don't think I want him to slow down Nai."

"Okay, like I said before this is your train wreck. I'm your sister, so you know I'll be there to help you through the wreckage."

When we stopped at a red light she grabbed and squeezed my hand. "Everything's gonna be fine."

"Can you guarantee that?" I flashed a sheepish grin at her.

She'd always been so much more together than me and I kind of envied that about my best friend. Not once had I been the one to give her any real, useful advice. Now that I thought about I probably always just gave out some pompous, self-righteous bullshit that she would never live by. Damn, I had to reevaluate myself. It was a possibility that Devin wouldn't like me once he really got to know me.

"No, I can't, but I love you." She grinned back at me before pulling off.

"I love your crazy ass too."

* * *

"Wow, is he ever going to leave." I was feeling impatient.

Hour number two was approaching and I was tired of just sitting in the car waiting.

We were following him on this particular day because I had caught the tail end of his phone conversation the day before. He was agreeing to meet the person that he was talking to after work. I was sure that it was the shameless hoe he was cheating on me with.

"What if he's doing his dirt inside? Didn't you say that ya'll used to do it in his office sometimes?"

Janai just had to remind me. At first it didn't really bother me, but when I thought about it, it was kind of fucked up. Damn, wasn't I young enough for him?

"In that case who is he meeting after work? If we go inside he'll see us, especially me. Maybe you should go inside. His name is on his office door," I suggested.

"He could've changed the plan, so I'm going in to see." Just as she was about to get out of the car I spotted him walking toward the parking lot. We weren't parked too far from his champagne colored Suburban.

"He's coming," I whispered.

She climbed back in the car and we waited for him to pull out of his parking space. It took him a while because it appeared that he was talking to somebody on the phone.

"He must be confirming his little date." It came out angrier than I meant for it to and of course Janai caught on.

"Are you jealous bitch? Let me find out," she teased.

"I'm not jealous." I rolled my eyes. "I'm just a little pissed that he would cheat on me. I mean, I'm way younger than him and I'm flyy. Shit, like Devin said, he's a fool."

"Right. His loss. Not yours. Let's just dig up this dirt and get this divorce going."

I nodded in agreement. "Okay. He's leaving now. Wait a few seconds before you pull off and don't follow him close."

Janai sucked her teeth. "Girl, you ain't gotta school me on how to follow somebody. I do this. You just sit back and ride."

I laughed. "Well, excuse me Sherlock Holmes."

She laughed and turned the radio on. Of course the music was blasting loud as hell with all of that trunk rattling bass.

"Damn," I shrieked and covered my ears.

She turned it down quickly.

"How the hell are we supposed to be following somebody making all that noise?" I asked.

Janai laughed. "I'm sorry. It's the first time I tuned the radio on since I been in the car. You know Reggie be having that shit pumping and shit."

"Yeah, just focus before we lose him in all this damn traffic."

"Yes ma'am," she said playfully.

I sighed because I wasn't really in a playful mood. Shit, I should've popped one more damn Xanax.

"I'm going to need a drink and a blunt after this."

"Whatever you need boo," Janai said just as Isaac pulled up to a Jamaican restaurant called The Golden Crust.

Hmm, that didn't seem like a place that he would frequent. I could see him getting carry out because it was near the school, but I couldn't imagine him meeting a woman there. Maybe he was just being low key, like Devin and I. That shit made me cringe.

Janai didn't park that close to him, but we were able to see what was going on once he was inside. He sat down at a booth close to the window and we had a good view of him. We sat there in silence waiting for something to happen. I was literally holding my breath.

"There's a woman sitting at the booth. Can you see her?" Janai asked.

I took a closer look and she was right. There was some chick across from him and then she suddenly moved to sit beside him. They shared a hug and I tried to get a better look at her, but it was hard to really make out her features.

"She doesn't even look that young. She looks about his age." Her skin was the same complexion as mine and she had long, bouncy hair, but she was clearly not that young. Was he cheating on me with someone closer to his age? I guess he was over the younger woman thing.

"You want to go in and confront them. Shit, we can because…"

"Nah, I'm just going to take some pictures of this shit and confront him about it when he comes home. Right now I just want to get that drink. I see what I need to see and confronting them now won't solve anything. I'm just going to get me a divorce lawyer and get them coins."

Janai put her hand out for a five. "That's what I'm talking about bitch. Hit him where it really hurts."

I slapped her five, pulled my Nikon camera out and zoomed in close enough so that Isaac and his woman friend were clearly in the picture. Maybe I needed a little more before I confronted him. They weren't really being lovey dovey and so he could lie about their relationship. Still, he was meeting with some woman.

"Do you think we should dig a little bit more? Maybe these pictures aren't going to be enough proof," I said as Janai pulled off.

"I mean, if you want to. You're just going to have to keep your mouth closed about what you already know. Maybe you should talk to her before you really hit him with it."

"You're right." My mind was full of all types of scenarios about meeting with his mistress myself.

What if she was crazy like Amil?

"Damn, let's go get that drink. You want to stop at a bar or go to my house?" Janai asked.

"Do you have some weed?"

She giggled. "You know I do."

"Your house then, maybe your neighbors will entertain us again."

We both laughed.

* * *

"Come home now! We need to talk!" Isaac's voice blared through the phone.

The audacity of his cheating ass to call yelling at me. "What the hell is this all about Isaac? I'm with Janai."

Did he want to confess his cheating ways? Was he finally ready to end our façade of a marriage? I knew that he was aware of the clause in our prenuptial agreement being that he had it drawn up himself. Maybe he was ready to give up those funds.

"I said we need to talk, so I expect for you to be on your way soon." With that said he hung up on me.

I just stared at the phone in disbelief like I'd get some type of explanation or something from it.

"What's wrong?" Janai asked in concern. "Was that Devin?"

I shook my head. "No, it was Isaac. He said we need to talk and I need to come home now."

"Hmm, maybe he's ready to confess and end the marriage. That might've been what his meeting with old girl was all about. Now you'll be free to finally do what you want. He has no choice but to pay up."

"Yeah, that's the same thing I was just thinking. I won't even have to argue with him. Let me get to the house and see what he has to say." I stood up feeling a little woozy from the joint we'd just smoked.

We'd also had some Patron shots and a taco salad that my girl had whipped up. That shit had hit the spot for real.

"Okay. Well, call me when you get there. Are you alright to drive?"

I steadied myself. "Yeah girl. I'm good." Shit, part of me wasn't so sure that I was.

She pulled me in for a hug. "Like I said before boo. Everything's going to be okay. It'll all work out. You two going forward with a divorce is best for the both of you."

"Yeah, I know. I just want what he owes me, that's all." I pulled away and my drunk ass friend had tears in her eyes. You'd think she was the one who'd just caught her husband cheating.

"I just hate to see you go through this bullshit. You're being strong, but I'm sure that it hurts at least a little. He's been your husband for almost eight years." She wiped her eyes and walked me to the door.

"I'm really okay Nai. I just know that something has to give. It's time for me to finally be happy with somebody and I think I can be with Devin. Well, if Amil stays in her damn place." I shook my head at the thought of her.

Maybe the fact that I had stood up for myself had made her fall back. Either that or she had found a man to move on with. Damn, I was hoping that both were true.

* * *

When I walked inside Isaac was waiting for me in the den. He was smoking a pipe with a large white envelope sitting in his lap. There was a glass full of vodka on the coffee table and I was sure that it wasn't his first drink.

"Sit down honey," he said with a pleasant smile on his face.

I was surprised that I had even made it home in one piece, so I didn't feel like playing guessing games.

"What is this all about?" I asked as flashbacks of what I'd seen earlier played in my mind. As bad as I wanted to say something I held it in as I sat down.

I wondered what was in the envelope. Part of me kind of felt that it held divorce papers. As I waited for him to answer I wondered how I would feel when he actually told me that he wanted to end our marriage. Would I feel anything?

"Well, I am not really surprised, but…" He opened the envelope and pulled out the contents.

As he laid it out on the table my mouth literally hit the floor. There were pictures of me and Devin at Janai's cabin at Lake Allatoona.

He continued. "I met with a private investigator today. After getting a phone call to spark my suspicions a couple weeks ago, I decided to have you followed."

I gulped. "Isaac…"

"It's no point in you saying anything. I have all the proof I need. Some woman just called me out of the blue talking about you're sleeping with her man. She sounded like she's from your old neighborhood."

That had to be that damn Amil. No wonder that ghetto ass hoe was acting all calm and shit. She had been plotting against me all along, but who the hell was the bitch that Isaac had met up with.

"You're talking about me cheating when I caught you all hugged up with some hoe today." With an attitude I pulled my camera out and showed him the pictures I'd taken. Shit, we were both cheating, so now what?

Damn, he had pictures of me and Devin kissing though. What I had was nothing next to his evidence. I was fucked and I knew it, but I was trying to find some kind of leverage to use. If only I'd had a child by him. That would've secured my future. He made sure to take that away from me.

"That's Tamia, she's the PI I hired. We went to school together." He chuckled and shook his head. "Did you even read the prenuptial agreement that you signed?"

So, that's whose card that was? I guess he hid it in the gun case for a reason. He thought I wouldn't look there. No wonder the card was blank. She was a PI and maybe it was good to keep that bit of information discreet. Then I wondered if the other number I'd highlighted was Amil's.

It was like I didn't even hear him talking anymore. My head was swimming. What the hell was I going to do? Of course I had read the prenuptial agreement. In the event that I cheated on him and he could prove it, I wouldn't even get twenty five percent of my business. I would be walking away from my fucked up marriage with absolutely nothing. I had been a fool to sign that shit. Ohhh, when I got my hands on that bitch Amil I was going to squeeze the life out of her.

My next thought was to try tears. Maybe I could get some sympathy from him if I threw in how he'd treated me over the years. Not only that, but his family had really made my life hell too.

"I'm sorry Isaac. I never meant to do anything to hurt you or us, but you have to admit that you haven't been a husband to me in years. Not only that, but your mother treats me like shit. Your daughter and her mother can't stand me and it shows." The tears fell from my eyes and I deserved an Academy Award for my performance.

He only smiled at me as if he was amused. "I have provided everything for you Fanci. If anything you should appreciate that. You shouldn't be complaining about anything because I'm the only man who has ever given a fuck about you. Your own father didn't even want your ass. My mother was right about you. You're a whore and I should've known not to fall for you. You signed a prenup, but you were still after my money. If you loved me you would've tried to work it out with me, but no, you just went and fucked some damn body. That's why you stood up to my mother and Lorraine. You'd never been that brave before. I see that the new dick in your life has given you some balls."

I was shocked by his words. "What? I do love you Isaac." I'd say whatever I needed to say for him not to just send me out there with nothing. He hadn't mentioned a divorce yet. Maybe I could get him to hold on until I was in a better financial situation. Maybe I could convince him that I would leave Devin alone.

There was no way that I was really going to do that. The two of us would just have to be a lot more careful about how we did things. How we would be able to accomplish that, I had no clue. Damn, I needed another Xanax.

"You don't mean this Isaac. I'm sorry. We can go to counseling and work this out…"

"You're just saying that because you're assed out. I hope your new boyfriend has somewhere for you to live. I'm filing for divorce in the morning and I want you out of my house. I'll make sure that you don't get a damn thing. You're leaving this marriage with what you came with bitch…Nothing!"

His voice was like a roar that I could feel in my soul. The vibration had rattled all over my body.

"Get out? But you have to give me some time." My own low voice trembled.

He stood up. "I don't have to give your cheating ass shit!"

My first thought was to drive to Janai's until he cooled off. I knew that he would cool off.

"Okay. I'll spend the night at Janai's. Just let me go get some clothes and I'll be on my way. We can talk about this tomorrow after you've calmed down."

He looked down at me with eyes that had turned red with anger. Either that or he'd had a few too many drinks.

"We have nothing to talk about and you don't have any clothes. I took them all to the dumpster. As a matter of fact you don't have shit.

Like I said, you're leaving like you came." He put his hand out. "Give me the key to my BMW."

When the tears fell that time they were real as hell. He was taking my damn car too?

"Come on Isaac. That's fucked up." Did he really throw all of my things in the dumpster? I started thinking about every outfit, shoe and piece of jewelry that I loved.

"You are not driving anywhere in anything that I pay for. You knew what would happen if you cheated on me."

I shook my head. "You've never loved me Isaac. Never. I was only something else for you to own."

After going through my purse I passed him my car key.

"Give me the house keys too," he said pointedly.

Damn, he was being really fucked up about it. I knew that I was wrong, but he knew that I had nowhere to go.

"What about my mother?" My voice cracked and he casted his eyes down.

"I'm giving you a week to figure it out before I kick her old, gold digging ass out too." He was being so wicked and I couldn't believe that I'd ever married him.

I grabbed the only purse that I had left and took out my cell phone to call Janai. Isaac just sat there and kept his eyes trained on me.

"Hello," Janai answered with a question in her voice.

I knew that she wanted a rundown of what had happened, but she just didn't know the half.

"Come pick me up please. I need to spend the night over there." My voice was flat because I didn't want to say anything until we were face to face.

"What? So, you told him that you know already?" She was ready to gossip, but I wasn't willing to in front of my soon to be ex-husband.

"Just come get me. We'll talk later."

"Okay, damn. I'm on my way."

I hung up the phone and he put his hand out again.

"You used your one phone call. Now give me my phone," he said with a snooty ass look on his face.

Ugghh, I hated him. "Are you serious right now Isaac? Really? You're taking my fucking phone? You're really being an ass right now."

"No, the point is you shared my ass with some street thug who has no ounce of education. I should've known. That's what the fuck you grew up around and...I should've left your ass in the hood where you belong."

My mouth was wide open. "Don't go there! I don't need you to talk down to me. I'm human Isaac! You didn't want this ass, so I figured why not, but I made a mistake okay and we can..."

"Shut the fuck up and give me my damn phone!" He picked up his glass of liquor, drained it and then threw it against the wall.

I jumped when it shattered and broke into pieces. I stared at the broken glass on the hardwood floor as I handed him the phone.

"Wait for your friend outside!" He yelled before leaving the room.

That fool has lost his damn mind.

Chapter 12

Devin

"Hold up babe, hold up, what did you say again?" I led a hysterically crying Fanci inside of my spot and closed the door.

She had just popped up at my door explaining something that I couldn't understand. All I heard her say was her husband had thrown her out with nothing. Did I hear her right? When she finally took a breath and calmed down enough so that I could comprehend, I was floored.

"So, that's why Amil's been actin' all nice and shit!" The thought of the shit storm she had started infuriated me.

"I promise you that I'm going to kill that bitch Devin! She has ruined my fuckin' life!" Fanci screamed in an angry fit.

Her eyes looked enraged and I don't think I'd ever seen her look like that. She didn't even look that mad when she threw the water in Amil's face at J. Christopher's. I had to calm her down so that she wouldn't be thinking about doing something stupid.

"I know that you're pissed Fanci and I am too, but you can't do anything crazy. She is the mother of my child and as fucked up as it is, I have to consider that." I grabbed her hand and kissed it.

She yanked her hand away and rolled her eyes. "Well, I don't."

I let out a sigh knowing that she was just in her feelings at the moment. There wasn't really much I could say to change how she felt. She needed some time to adjust to the change that her life was about to take. Her comfort zone had been tampered with thanks to Amil and I understood her anger. Still, I was kind of glad that things were finally moving forward because we could be together.

"Look on the bright side babe. We can be together now…"

She just broke out into hysterical laughter like a crazy person. One minute she was crying and the next she was acting like she had heard the funniest joke of her life.

"We can be together now? How old are you again Devin?" She stopped laughing and shook her head. "Your ass is over there in a fantasy world, but I'm dealing with reality. I don't have shit other than the clothes on my back and you're talking about we can be together. Add the fact that you have a connection with a crazy bitch that you have to deal with for the rest of your life. My life is going downhill fast and you're looking on the bright side. Where the fuck is the bright side of this shit? It didn't happen the way it was supposed to Devin. How the fuck are we just going to be together? Like it would be that damn simple!"

"Damnit Fanci, you sound real fuckin' selfish right now. Was this just a fuck thing because you can't seem to see past what you've lost? What about what you'll be gaining now. I love you! He didn't. I can provide a life for you. Unlike him, I can make you happy and I want to. What the hell ma?" I shook my head in confusion.

There she was bitching about how she had nothing. Damn, at least she still had me. The situation with Amil was fucked up, but we could work past all of that. Why was she making me feel like I wasn't enough although she had ran straight to me?

She sighed and ran her fingers through her hair. "I'm sorry Devin. Okay. Shit, I've just been through hell. I do care about you and I know that you can make me happy, because you have. Still, I'm used to a certain type of lifestyle and with everything that you already have going on, you can't provide that for me. I even have my mother to take care of. He's giving me a week to figure out where she's going to go." Tears were welling up in her eyes again. "I'm a complete failure and…"

I walked over to her and folded her into my chest for an embrace. "We'll figure it out baby. You got me. I ain't goin' nowhere. I already told you how I feel about you. I got you."

"You make it sound so simple," she moaned in defeat.

I pulled away from her. "Look at me. I said I got you and it's that fuckin' simple. Okay?"

She nodded as I wiped her tears away. "No more crying. I'll get you a car tomorrow so you can get around and you can stay with me as long as you want to."

"Until you get some control over Amil I'll be staying at Janai's. Since you insist on me not killing the bitch."

I nodded before kissing her pouted lips. "Okay, but for now I want you to relax and try to get your mind off what happened."

She sighed. "How can I do that? My mind is stuck on what happened. I'm so upset with both Isaac and Amil. You just don't know the thoughts that are floating around in my head. I honestly don't think I'll be able to relax anytime soon."

"You sure?" I asked with a grin and then kissed her neck.

To most it wouldn't seem like the time to try to do something sexual to her. Sex also would only be a temporary fix, but at least it would take her mind and body somewhere else for a little while. I didn't know if she'd even be down for it, but at the moment I couldn't think of anything else to do to relieve her stress.

"I'm not in the mood." She gently pushed me away and I didn't push the issue.

"Okay," I breathed. "How about I run you a nice, hot bubble bath?"

Her eyes suddenly lit up at least a little bit. "That sounds good."

I stood up without saying another word and headed to the master bath. The huge garden tub had jets like a Jacuzzi, so she could try to unwind a little bit. My hope was that she'd find it in her heart to trust me. I was the type of man who planned and if she would just be patient with me I would come up with a way to make everything alright.

That point in time wasn't the right one to have that conversation with her. Everything that had happened was too fresh. In time I would handle

Amil and come up with a way to accommodate Fanci's mother. I didn't make billions, but my income was in the six figures. If I budgeted right I could make it happen. I had been wanting to buy a house anyway. If we could find her mother a temporary place to stay I'd be able to buy a house and let her mother stay in the condo.

After I turned on the water, I poured in a little sweet smelling bubble bath that Gina had left at my spot. It was by Bath and Body Works. A few months ago she had to stay at my crib for a few days while her apartment was being painted. I was glad she'd left that shit, because it had come in handy.

"Okay baby, your bubble bath is ready," I said as I stood at the foot of the bed.

She gave me a look that let me know that she still didn't feel any better about her situation. As she slowly sat up on the bed, I reached over and grabbed her hand. I needed her to know that I would hold her down and uplift her when she needed it. Maybe the lack of real love in her life was the reason she held on to material things so tightly. If only she'd hold on to me like she was holding on to the money that she was not going to get from her husband. At least I wasn't planning on going anywhere.

"C'mon Fanci," I coaxed.

She finally stood up and let me lead her into the bathroom. The steam was rising from the water as I helped her undress.

"Get on in while it's hot babe."

She was being unusually quiet and it made me feel very uneasy.

"You okay?" I asked.

It was hard to hold a conversation by myself, so I needed her to talk to me.

Fanci nodded. "I will be. I just need some time to come up with something."

I didn't know exactly what she meant by that. After trying to reassure her that I was there for her she still seemed to feel like she was on her own. I guess my actions would just have to speak louder than my words.

"I told you I got you, but if you must try to come up with the solution on your own let me know what you come up with…okay." Yeah, I was getting a little frustrated, but I had to try to understand.

She just looked up at me with an annoyed smirk on her face. "Do you really think you're helping right now?"

"Probably not, but I *am* trying. That's a lot more than the nigga you're married to was doing." I sighed and balled up my fists.

Without saying another word Fanci stepped into the water and turned on the jets. "You're absolutely right," she said in a sad voice as she sat down.

"Do you want me to stay in here with you or do you need some time alone?" I had to look outside of my feelings for her and understand that she'd just been dumped by her husband.

No matter what she did or said, that shit had to be devastating. Her marriage was over and that had to make her feel like she'd failed. Add on top of that the fact that she would be getting nothing out of her pain and suffering. That shit was fucked up and my heart actually went out to her.

"Honestly Devin, I want to be alone for a little while. I need to think. It's like I just can't think straight right now."

I wanted to tell her that I loved her and I wanted her to tell me that she loved me back, but I knew that the timing was all wrong.

"Shit, I just hope that bitch Amil doesn't show up because with the way I feel I'm sure I'd murder that vindictive, hood rat ass hoe." Her face was all balled up and I'd never seen her look like that.

I cleared my throat. "She won't. Just try to chill bae. I hate to see you all fucked up like this. I for one don't get no kind of pleasure out of seeing you in pain."

"Can you just leave now?" She asked. "I'm not in the mood for any of that lovey dovey shit."

Damn, so she wanted to use her words as weapons against me. That was just a defense mechanism. She really wanted to lash out at Isaac and Amil, but she couldn't so she was taking that shit out on me. I cared for Fanci, so I would just roll with the punches, but damn, why the fuck did she come over? To punish *me* for our sin?

I let out a heavy sigh and closed the door behind me after leaving the bathroom. If she wanted some time alone, I would grant her that. She had come to me for a reason and I would allow her to treat me like shit if it would make her feel better.

Like I'd said before, there was nothing that I wouldn't do to make sure that I had Fanci in my life. I had been determined since the moment I saw her and so I wasn't going to give up that easily.

* * *

"I'm in the mood now," Fanci's voice was low and flirtatious as she stood in the bathroom's doorway.

The darkness of my bedroom caused her sexy, naked silhouette to stand out with the light from the bathroom as a backdrop.

Suddenly I had second thoughts about having sex with her. Something told me that she was too vulnerable and maybe I should do something else.

"Come here baby."

She sashayed toward me and then leaned over to give me a kiss. Damn, I wanted her so bad, but that shit was redundant. Shit had suddenly become real as hell and I had to take it seriously. Did I really want to be with Fanci on a long term basis? Was I really ready for us to live together?

"I want you to lie down on your stomach," I instructed before going to get the Bath & Body Works lotion to rub her down with.

"Why do you have all of this feminine, smelly good stuff?" She asked after I came back in the room.

"Although most people don't think it's possible, I have a best friend who is a female. She stayed over here for a few days not too long ago while her place was being painted and…"

"So, have you ever had sex with her?" I couldn't see her face, so I had no idea what her facial expression was.

"No, I haven't. She's like my sister and…"

"So, you have *never* wanted to have sex with her?"

"No, I haven't."

My ears were hot, because when I first met Gina I *was* attracted to her. Lying wasn't easy for a nigga who was as real as me. I usually kept it one hundred, but when it came to Fanci, I'd say whatever I had to say to keep her. I'd questioned being with her on a long term basis, but I had to admit that I was deeply in love with her. Neither of us had planned it, but it happened anyway.

"If you say so," she closed her eyes.

I poured lotion in my hands, rubbed them together to warm it and then started to rub her body down beginning with the back of her neck.

"Mmm, that feels sooooo good," she moaned.

Her skin felt so soft and smooth and the lotion was making it feel like butter.

"Damn Fanci, mmm mmm mmm," I said as my hands moved down her back.

"I told you that I was ready to…"

"Just let me do this first baby. I need to do this right now." I wasn't a sucker, but I wanted her to know that I was more than just a fling. I poured more lotion in my hands and repeated the process.

"Okay." She exhaled. "Mmm, this massage is better than any I've ever paid for."

I let out a light chuckle that was meant to sound sexy, but I didn't know if I'd pulled it off.

"Your pussy is better than any I've ever paid for," I said playfully.

She laughed and it was good to see that she was loosening up even if it was just for a short moment.

"You've paid for pussy before?" She asked. "Not as in prostitution right?"

My laughter filled the space of the room as my hands traveled down to her round ass cheeks. Damn, I loved her ass.

"Nah babe, I was fuckin' wit' you. I ain't never been with a prostitute. If I paid for it she was probably just a gold digger."

"You're crazy, but I needed this massage. I'm finally starting to relax."

"Good." I genuinely felt like it was all good as long as she knew that I was there for her.

"Baby, I have a solution to all of our problems, but I don't know how you will feel about it," Fanci's voice was suddenly serious.

"Spill it." My hands had moved down to her thick thighs.

"Well...Isaac has a life insurance policy for half a million and it states that if he dies his ex-wife and I will split that. We're both beneficiaries."

So, where was the conversation going? I wasn't really feeling it. She continued without me even having to ask.

"Help me kill him. We have to do it before he contacts a divorce lawyer, because then I will definitely be the first suspect."

It was as if she'd figured it all out, but what she didn't know was I wasn't with murdering anybody. In that case I would've killed Amil a long time ago, but I'd managed not to do that shit. I wasn't going to risk going back to prison for anybody. I was on parole and if I committed a murder that would be my ass. Not only that, but I wanted to get custody of my daughter. I loved Fanci, but she wasn't worth me losing that chance.

"You can't be serious baby..."

"I'm so serious," she cut me off. "I don't think I've ever been so serious about something in my life. We could set it up to look like a robbery...and...I mean...I can't just do it myself. You know I'd be the first suspect. I thought about using his gun to do it myself, but...that would be too obvious."

Wow, was she really serious, or just in her feelings and talking crazy. My hands moved down to her calves.

"You don't mean any of that baby. You're just talking right now. Besides, I was a jack boy, not a murderer. I love you, but I can't agree to kill nobody ma. I'm already on parole and I'm trying to get my daughter yo'. I can't risk that." Damn, I couldn't believe that she had actually considered murder as an option.

"Yeah, you're right. That's crazy. I'm just…fuck it. Forget I said it." She let out a sigh as I rubbed her feet.

Shit, after that I didn't know how to feel. We'd just literally had pillow talk about killing her husband. What the fuck? I knew that her head was fucked up, but murder was a whole different level of crazy. We'd been through a lot in a short amount of time and I didn't want to give up on her. However, the way she was talking was making me wonder what kind of state of mind she was in. Should I sleep with one eye open?

After I was done with her massage I glanced over at the clock. It was approaching four am and I for one needed some sleep. My dick wasn't anywhere near hard after everything that had happened and the shit she'd just presented to me. All I wanted to do was get some sleep.

"It's forgotten ma." I playfully slapped her on the ass. "Let's get some rest okay."

She nodded. "K. I am tired."

I snuggled up to her naked body. "Do you want a tee shirt or something? I'll give you some money to go shopping when we get up."

"No, I'm fine just like this. Just hold me." She sniffed like she was crying again.

I kissed her cheek lightly. "Okay baby. You know that I love you right. No matter what."

"Mmm hmm and I love you too Devin."

Next thing I knew she was snoring lightly and I was out like a light soon after.

Chapter 13

Fanci

I woke up the next morning feeling refreshed and accepting of what had happened. It wasn't meant for me to be with Isaac and I strongly believed that Devin was really my soulmate. It was obvious because we'd both fallen for each other so fast. He was from my old neighborhood, so I was supposed to meet him a long time ago. Devine intervention had done that later in life and I had to do whatever possible to secure myself in his life and financially.

My feelings about killing my husband hadn't changed. It was just a mistake to try to bring Devin into it. I didn't want him to risk his freedom and getting custody of his daughter for me. I had to just take care of it myself and make sure that the both of us were in the clear. That way I could ensure that we were together. Hopefully he would get his daughter and we'd have a child. I wanted a family so bad. Isaac had taken that away from me, but with Devin I had that chance.

As far as Amil, I didn't know what to do with that bitch. She had it coming though and I would come up with something for her too. I couldn't let her get away with doing what she had did. She had no right to contact Isaac about my affair with Devin. How did she find out about him anyway? The hoe was on some other shit and being that she had sent for me, I was coming for her ass. I was so tired of being classy and refined. The real Fanci was about to bust out and take care of everybody who had violated me.

"Morning babe," Devin said in a sweet voice as she looked up at me.

The look in his eyes was questioning like he was wondering if I was over killing Isaac. He looked so damn concerned that I just had to put him at ease.

"Morning babe. Don't worry. I was in my feelings and...I didn't mean any of that shit about...you know." I tried to play innocent like I couldn't repeat such nonsense.

He smiled that gorgeous smile. "Good, 'cause I was like what the fuck?"

I smiled back, but my smile wasn't genuine. "Let's just act like that conversation never happened. Okay."

He nodded in agreement. "No problem baby. There's nothing that I would like to do more."

"Are you sure?" I asked sexily.

His smile faded. "Well, I do have one thing in mind."

I giggled as he positioned his body on top of mine.

"Wit' yo' fine ass," he said in a low voice.

My body was on fire and I needed some type of distraction from reality. Sex was like a drug and the release of dopamine in my brain was exactly what I needed. The Xanax wasn't working to curb my desire to do something erratic and part of me was a little scared of what I was thinking.

Still, I had to do me. I was used to living a certain lifestyle and I just couldn't go back to my former life. Shit, the thought of struggling frightened the shit out of me. So, I went with the moment hoping that after Devin made love to me, I'd change my mind about being a murderer.

When he entered me slowly, I gasped. He hadn't bothered to put on a condom and honestly we'd slipped up before. Neither of us seemed to care about the consequences of that because our attraction was just so strong. I was already super wet, so the contact of our bodies grinding and moving in sync put me exactly where I needed to be. At ease.

"Mmm…ahhhh…Devin…you know exactly what to do to my body…uhhh…damn…" He kissed my words away and I felt that life was finally about to make a turn for the better.

I still wanted to off Isaac's ass though.

* * *

Later that day Devin took me to the dealership to get a brand new silver BMW. After that he took me on a shopping spree, but it still wasn't enough. I was thinking about my closet at Isaac's and the items he'd admitted to getting rid of. One little shopping spree couldn't compare to that, but I was grateful for the car.

Once we got back to his place I was ready to put my plan into motion. I had been pondering about it all day.

"I need to go to the office for a few hours babe and then after that I'll probably go to Janai's. Honestly, with the way I'm feeling I don't want to run into *her* ass."

He knew that I was referring to Amil, so he nodded in agreement. "Okay ma. I'm gonna talk to her and shit. It's time to move forward with getting custody of Londyn. Uh, how do you feel about that?"

"I love children Devin and I have always wanted a family. If you're open to having more children later I'm fine with that too." I smiled as I grabbed my purse.

He was grinning all big and it just warmed my heart to think about what the future would bring. I didn't want to be one of those chicks who just mooched off him and didn't have shit to bring to the table. I wanted one hundred percent of my business and at least six figures in my bank account. At that point I only had twenty five thousand saved up. I hadn't told Devin about that. My mother needed me and no matter what she did or said, I wanted to make sure that she was taken care of. She had done that for me despite the fact that my sorry ass father didn't want me.

* * *

When I got in the car I called my cousin Rod on the cell phone that Devin had bought for me. I was grateful for that shit too. It was a good thing that I had memorized his number and Janai's. They were really the only people I talked to her other than my mom and of course her number was embedded in my brain.

"Sup cuz?" He asked. I could hear the sound of some loud ass music in the back ground.

"Nothing much." Although Rod was still in our old hood doing the same old thing, we'd always kept in touch. We were close as kids, so despite my instinct to leave the past behind, I'd held on to him for some reason.

"Auntie told me 'bout old dude and shit. That's fucked up, but I knew that shit wasn't gon' last."

"It's whatever. I need to come through and talk to you about something."

He knew killers and all I needed was to present my scheme, pay the right person and get it over with. All I wanted to do was move on with my life and fast.

"A'ight, but I don't know the last time you ventured into the hood. This must be serious."

"Dead ass," I added before putting on a pair of dark Ray Ban's that covered most of my face.

"I'll be here." With that said he hung up.

* * *

I hadn't been at Rod's for five seconds and I was ready to leave. It was such a small, cramped up space full of thug ass dudes. They were playing a video game on the big screen TV, cursing all loud and smoking blunts full of some good smelling weed.

"Can I get some of what they smoking?" I asked him.

He gave me a surprised look as the thick weed smoke wafted around the tiny space.

"Damn cuzzo. That shit must be really getting to you," he said with a snicker.

"Fuck you Rod." I couldn't help but laugh too as he passed me a baggie of lime green buds.

"So, what's really up? I know you ain't come all the way here for no damn weed." His face was serious and there was no hint of humor in his voice.

"I need you to get somebody to…" I cleared my throat. "Take care of Isaac for me."

"You sure. Once it's done it's done," he stated.

I nodded with conviction. "Hell yeah I'm sure. I will pay. I just need the shit to look random and it has to happen asap. Like tomorrow."

"Wow cuz, that soon?" He looked skeptical.

"Hell yeah. Well, late tomorrow night. I can tell you exactly where he'll be. It can't be at the house. You have to make sure it looks random. On Friday nights he goes to his only friend Gary's house to play Poker and drink. He always leaves at around one am. Maybe we can have him followed and then...you know. He usually wins and has a lot of cash on him. Rob him, take his Rolex and his car. That way that shit doesn't fall on me." After it was out I still didn't feel bad about it. I needed that shit done.

"I'm gonna ask you one more time? Are you sure?" Rod's eyes were stuck on mine.

"I'm so sure." I didn't break our eye contact as I reached into my purse and pulled out five thousand in cash. "This is half. The other half will be delivered when it's done and I need proof that it's done. Make it happen Rod."

He nodded. "A'ight cuz. Already."

"You'll know his Suburban and what he looks like right?" I asked just to be sure.

He hadn't seen Isaac in years so I wanted to be sure.

"Yeah, I know that nigga when I see him."

I nodded and we shook on it. "Okay. I have to go to the office for a little while. Be in touch. You have my new number."

He gave me a tight hug. "Keep your head up

"Of course. Always. You know that." I was glad to finally walk out and get some fresh air.

The thought of my plan falling into place made me smile as I walked toward my new car.

* * *

Devin

"You have really gone too far this time Amil. What the fuck is wrong wit' your ass? Just move on wit' your life ma. I don't want you." I shook my head as I paced back in forth outside of my tattoo shop.

She laughed. "You knew I wasn't gonna let that bitch get away with puttin' her fuckin' hands on me right? Besides, I thought I told you that I was going to trace her license plate number. I have connections and I can find out anything I want. Her car was in her husband's name, so I got his information and then called him. What happened, did he kill the bitch? I hope so." Her laugh was a wicked cackle.

"That's shit ain't funny woman. I swear you get crazier by the day. It's really sad. I feel sorry for you."

"Nah nigga. I feel sorry for your ass. You're the one who is taking care of me. I'm sitting back enjoying the fruits of your labor while I do what the fuck I wanna do. To be honest, this shit's not even about you. I don't even think I want you. I just don't want you wit' anybody else."

I just shook my head because I knew that I couldn't get through to her. "I can't talk to you right now. You being petty as hell and I ain't got time for it. I got work to do. Just know that I petitioned the court for custody so…"

She cut me off real quick. "Bye Craig! You will never get Londyn. Believe that shit."

I was nonchalant about it. "We'll see ma. We'll see."

I ended the call and went back in the shop to take care of my next appointment. Before the door could even close good some dude stepped in all quick behind me. He was on my heels so I turned around to tell his ass to back the fuck up.

Before I could get the words out his fist connected with my face. What the fuck? Who the hell was he? One of Amil's niggas?"

I got my bearings and started going into that nigga with uppercuts to the face and all types of body blows. At that point he seemed overwhelmed and when I noticed his features it was obvious that he was an older man. Was that Fanci's husband?

"You're fucking my wife," he finally said to confirm just that. "And I want you to leave her the fuck alone."

Finally two of the other male tattoo artists who worked there came over to break us up.

"Get the fuck out of my place of business wit' that shit! If I'm fuckin' your wife it's 'cause she wants it!"

He tried to fight his way out of the grasp of the two men, but they were too strong.

"Fuck you! I'll make sure your thugged out ass get exactly what you deserve! How dare you…"

"I'll kill yo' old ass. Get him the hell outta here!" I yelled before storming off to my office in anger.

* * *

"You gotta be kidding me baby. I'm so sorry," Fanci said sweetly after I filled her in on my little scuffle with her husband.

"If he was so ready to move the hell on why the fuck did he show up at my shop ready to get his old ass whooped?"

"Pride I guess," she offered as an explanation.

"Whatever. He gon' get his old ass fucked up messing wit' me. I'm just glad it was broken up before the police got involved. I ain't got time for that."

"I know." She sighed loudly.

"It's crazy, because I had just got off the phone wit' Amil's psycho ass before that shit happened. Enough about our exes. We'll be together soon. So, what you got going on tomorrow. It's a Friday night, so I figured we could just chill and watch a movie at the crib or something."

She cleared her throat. "Sorry love. I have plans with Janai tomorrow. We're going to the Tabernacle to see D'Angelo and then we're going to get some drinks. I'll see you on Saturday. Okay."

I was disappointed, but I understood the distance. Amil's presence wasn't too appealing and she probably needed some girls' time instead of laying up with me.

"Okay cool. Saturday it is ma. Love you."

"Love you too babe. I'll call you when I get to Janai's."

"Okay."

"Try to stay out of trouble. I'm sorry that my past has caught up with us. Don't worry. His bark is more dangerous than his bite. He'll go away eventually," she said referring to Isaac.

"Hmm, he better, because my business and freedom could be in jeopardy."

"I'm sure it won't come to that. We'll just get the divorce over with and then the two of us can be together. Well, that's if Amil's out of the way." Her voice sounded malicious.

"Don't start talking crazy again…"

"I'm not. I don't mean murder or anything Devin damn. I told you what that was all about. I'm just saying that I wish your ex would just find her own man. You're mine."

"Okay ma. I have a client to get to. Talk to you later sexy."

"Okay baby."

We ended the call and I tried to push the fight with her husband and Amil out of my mind.

Chapter 14

Fanci

Before I went out with Janai I met up with my mother at The Cheesecake Factory on Peachtree Rd. in Buckhead. It was time for us to talk about my financial crisis and how it affected her in the short term. The long term would be for me to collect the insurance money from Isaac's death and be able to take care of the both of us. In the meantime she needed to be prepared for anything.

"Hey mommy." I kissed her cheek and sat down.

"Hi honey. I ordered a sweet tea with lemon for you. The server should be over with our drinks and some bread soon. How are you holding up?" She gave me a sympathetic look.

Without knowing all of the details she managed to be on my side. She didn't know about the prenup or the fact that I had cheated. I was surprised that Isaac didn't tell her.

I shrugged my shoulders. "I'm okay. It's not like he's the first man to reject me and break my heart."

Being an only child had been a benefit for me. My mother spoiled the shit out of my ass and upheld me for everything. At the moment I needed her attention more than ever. I just hoped she wouldn't blame me for not keeping my marriage intact.

"You'll be fine baby. Isaac's family is rich and I'm sure that he will take good care of you."

The thought of what she was thinking infuriated me, but I kept my cool. She said he'd take care of me, but she meant us. It was sad that I seemed to be stuck taking care of a forty six year old woman. She'd given birth to me at the age of eighteen and now I guess it was my turn to take care of her already.

Before I could say anything else the server put our bread and drinks in front of us.

"Are you ready to order?" The tall, slim, white brunette asked with a smile.

"Not yet. Give us about ten minutes," I suggested with a cordial smile.

"Okay," she agreed before walking off.

"Mom, I think not knowing my father has affected me. Well, that's what my therapist kept telling me when I was going to her. I need to know why he didn't want me."

She gave me a look that let me know that I had struck a nerve. "Fuck him. He wasn't there and so we didn't need him. Besides, this isn't the time or place to talk about that."

I was irritated with her. "Just tell me something ma. Was he married? I mean, what? You were a beautiful woman and I can't see why he wasn't…married to you."

She sighed and spread butter onto a piece of bread. "Your daddy was also your uncle Fanci. My sister's ex-husband is your father. He started molesting me when I was seven and raped me when I was seventeen. I had you not too long after my eighteenth birthday. He was married to my sister Frances when I used to live with them. He was twenty five when he started molesting me and thirty five when he got me pregnant. They're not together anymore because of what he did. That's why you've never known him."

I was shocked and my jaw had literally hit the floor. So, the man that she said was my father was not. She had shown me pictures and everything. He was probably one of her ex-boyfriends. It was downright sick that a man would do that to a little girl and then rape her when she was a teenager.

My mom had told me that her mother died when she was six from lung cancer and she was sent to live with her only sister Frances who was Rod's mother. She was fifteen years older than my mom. That meant that Rod and I were first cousins and siblings. Damn. They were pregnant at the same time because Rod and I were the same age.

"Wow," I breathed. "I can't believe that."

"Hmm, baby girl, you'll be surprised about the things I've been through. I didn't tell you because I didn't want you to hold the burden of all of that. I was just waiting for the right time to tell you. I just hope you can handle it now." She sipped her drink and avoided making eye contact with me.

To be honest I couldn't handle it, but what choice did I really have? What had happened happened and it explained why my life had been the way it was. My family was small and now I understood why. Mom didn't really deal with Francis and it all made sense now. I guess she had blamed my mother when it was really her man's fault. He was the damn adult in the situation. No wonder I was so fucked up.

* * *

Later that night I got sexy as hell and went out with my best friend. It was perfect because not only did we have a ball, but I also had an alibi. As I listened to an out of shape D'Angelo sing "How

Does It Feel", I thought about Devin and his sexy body. It definitely felt good to have a man in my life like him.

He had handled me so well the night that I popped up at his condo. I had begged Janai to drop me off over there although she was skeptical about it. Instead of getting pissed off at me, or trying to get some ass, he went out of his way to make me feel better and I appreciated that.

"Damn, D'Angelo ain't as fine as he used to be," Janai said. "I mean, he's still cute, but he's a little pudgy. That don't matter though because he still sounds good."

I nodded. "Yup. He sounds damn good."

Then my thoughts drifted to what was supposed to go down later. Finally I was going to be free from my stifling marriage to Isaac. I wasn't an evil person, but I had to admit that I was selfish as well as self-serving. My mind had been made up and the ball was already in motion. I just hoped my cousin and his crew would be smart and clean about it. Shit, I didn't need anybody snitching on me in the case that they got caught.

* * *

It was almost two am and I was anxious. Rod still hadn't contacted me and I was wondering if Isaac had skipped his poker night at Gary's. The way that shit had been going lately I wouldn't doubt it one bit. I tried to hold it together as Janai and I left the bar at the Ritz Carlton. We'd gotten spoiled by some dudes who was generous with the free drinks. I made sure that I ordered something though so that I'd have a receipt with the time on it. That would only help if Rod had come through.

"I'm drunk as hell bitch, you sure you can drive?"

"I'm good bitch. Now buckle up your seatbelt and take a damn nap."

I laughed. "Shit, not the way you drive."

Suddenly my phone notified me that I had a message. I looked down at my phone and noticed that Rod had sent me a picture message.

When I stared at the picture my heart dropped. There Isaac was in the front seat of his Suburban with a bullet hole in his head. He looked dead and I was sure that he was, but I had to make sure that my cousin wasn't being reckless.

Me: Did you do it yourself?

Rod: Nah, got my nigga Rich to do it.

Me: Was you with him?

Rod: Hell yea.

Me: Ok. I'm about to delete this pic. Make sure you delete it too. And these messages.

Rod: Ok cuz. I'll call you tomorrow to let you know where to meet me.

Me: K. Thanks

Rod: Already

I looked away from the phone and noticed that Janai was concentrating on the road. For once I was speechless because my feelings were mixed. At one point in my life I wanted a future with Isaac. At one point I really cared for him. He had done me wrong and for that reason and that reason only, he'd gotten his karma. I didn't know if I'd get mine as well, but for the time being I was ready for the payout.

* * *

Being that I wasn't in the household anymore I was sure that I would find out about Isaac's death from one of his family members.

"Isaac was found dead not far from Gary's house," Iris cried into the phone.

"What?" I asked pretending to be surprised. I let out some sobs for emphasis, but no tears were falling. "Found dead? Was it an accident? Had he been drinking?"

"No," she cried. "He was robbed at gun point and shot according to the police. I just identified his body. You was his next of kin, but your phone was off and you wasn't at the house. Where are you?"

So, he hadn't told his mother about my affair or his plan to divorce me. That made me wonder if he was really going to go through with it.

I let the acting begin. "I've been out of town and I had no clue. Uh, I got a new number a few days ago. Oh my God. I can't believe this."

Fifteen minutes after I ended that call the police was at Janai's door. She was at work, so without hesitation I opened it. I was ready for whatever they had to say. My husband was dead and that was exactly what I had wanted, but I had to pretend that it wasn't.

I had no clue how they knew where to find me. Iris couldn't have told them and they got there that fast. Of course they were going to question me although it appeared to be a robbery. They had to rule me out as a suspect anyway and I was prepared for that.

"Can I help you officers?" I asked pretending not to know about Isaac's murder.

"Yes, I'm Detective Rodman and this is my partner Detective Newton. Are you Mrs. Fanci Moore?"

"Yes I am," I said as I stared up at them anxiously. "Is everything okay?"

"I don't know how to tell you this ma'am," Detective Newton spoke up. "But your husband was found early this morning. He was murdered. One gunshot wound to the head."

Tears fell from my eyes and I wailed like a wounded child. The two men just gave me sympathetic looks, but didn't attempt to touch or console me. I wiped my eyes and then calmed down a little. My sobs were still affecting them, I could tell by the way they kept looking at one another.

"Oh my God," I shrieked. "Who would murder Isaac?"

"That's what we're trying to figure out. We need you to come to the station to answer a few questions for us. It's just procedure."

I nodded. "Okay. Uh, just let me put on some shoes."

They agreed and I walked away from the door to put on some shoes and grabbed my purse. I was still pretending to be distraught as I walked to my car to follow the detectives to the station. I was just hoping that my crying fit and my alibi would make their suspicions disappear completely.

* * *

"So, where were you between the hours of ten pm and 2 am?" Detective Rodman asked with a stern look on his face.

He was an intimidating dark skinned man with severe features. Not only that, but he was pretty tall and built. Still, I was sticking to my guns and they hadn't accused me of murder…yet. I had to make sure they didn't.

"I went out with my best friend. We went to see D'Angelo perform at the Tabernacle and then we went to a bar after that." I wasn't crying all loud anymore, but I'd let some tears fall ever so often to throw them off.

I was so good at playing the innocent role because I looked the part. Men usually fell for my lies and I hoped that the Detectives would too.

However, if they put a woman on me, she'd probably see right through my ass. For some reason women just didn't like me.

"Do you have any proof that you were there?" His facial expression seemed to soften at the sight of my tearful, doe like eyes.

"Yes, as a matter of fact I have my ticket stub and receipt from the bar in my purse. I'm sure that you can check to see that I was there for sure." I kept eye contact with him the entire time.

He nodded. "Okay. Well, let me take a look."

I only looked away to look inside of my purse. "Thank God I didn't clean this purse out. I normally throw this type of stuff away." The little sniffles that I added after the statement hopefully drove it home that I didn't intend to keep proof of my alibi and it had just happened that way.

Detective Rodman looked at the ticket stub and the receipt carefully to make sure that they were authentic. "Okay, we will look into this and talk to your friend Janai as well. Do you know of anybody who would want to hurt your husband?"

I looked at him without missing a beat. "No, I can't think of one person who would want to hurt my husband. You said that it was a robbery right?"

"Yes, it appeared to be, but in some cases those instances are staged to throw the investigation off. Because of that theory we have to explore every possibility in order to pursue a suspect. You do understand that right?" He put his hands together on top of the table.

"Uh, yes, I do understand that Detective. I'm just shook up. I don't want to think about him being…murdered either way, but thinking of someone doing that to him…" I started crying again and the other Detective passed me a tissue. "I'm sorry. I just can't think about somebody doing that to Isaac because they wanted to murder him specifically. It had to be random because everybody loves Isaac. Oh my God, poor Megan. She's going to be so…" I shook my head and the tears started pouring again.

"That is all for now Mrs. Moore. We will check into you whereabouts and be in touch with you soon about the investigation. Please tell your friend to give us a call," Detective Newton chimed in.

He had been quiet the entire time. He was a white man with a slight tan, dark brown eyes and dark hair. I nodded and took the card that he was passing me from his hand. "Okay. I will."

As I sashayed out of the police precinct I couldn't help but think about how easy that was. It wasn't anything like the interrogations on cop shows that I had seen on television. I knew that I wasn't out of the clear yet and had to wait for them to confirm my alibi, but I wasn't really worried about it. In my eyes, I'd gotten away with murder.

When I got in my car my thoughts drifted to that bitch Amil. Now what was I going to come up with for her conniving, plotting ass. It was my time to plot and I wanted to do something that would ruin her and assure that Devin got full custody of their daughter. Then it occurred to me and I had the perfect way to do it.

* * *

Over the next couple days I did some snooping around when I was at Devin's to find out Amil's personal information. I had her address, full name and Londyn's full name. My common sense told me not to be at Devin's like that because the police were probably watching me. I didn't want our relationship to be exposed just yet.

I had got the maid Linda to let me in the house and I found that all of my things were intact in the master bedroom. A twinge of guilt had come over me because it was a possibility that Isaac wasn't going to divorce me. But would that have been a good thing. I was actually sick and tired of being married to him.

Devin had been very attentive to me and was helping me through my "grieving" process.

"I feel so bad baby. Just knowing that I thought about it and it happened makes me feel like I put it out there in the universe," I had cried on his shoulder the day before.

"Nah baby," he had consoled me. "It's not your fault at all. Shit happens sometimes okay."

If only he knew.

I was sitting in my car right outside of Janai's house when I made the call to DFCS.

"Dekalb Country Family and Children Services how can I help you?" A female asked.

"Yes, I'd like to make a report about an unfit mother, but can I remain anonymous?" I asked just to be sure.

"Yes you can. We keep all of our sources anonymous when we investigate claims," she explained. "You just give us any information that you have and we look into it to be sure if there is any truth to it. It's all about protecting innocent children. They don't ask to be in those situations and they can't get out of them without help. So, let me know what you're calling for."

Chapter 15

Devin

Almost a month had passed since the murder of Fanci's husband and Amil had also suddenly stopped harassing us. I figured she had finally decided to move on. The only thing was she was also not letting me see my daughter at all. I guess that was her new way of getting at me. All of that seemed to be about to make a turn when I got a call from DFCS about a complaint against her that they were investigating.

I was very cooperative and it worked in my favor being that I had filed for custody of Londyn right before the complaint was made.

"We are investigating the matter and will notify you of a court date if there are any findings. We want to make sure that your daughter is in the best possible home for her to grow up into a healthy, functioning adult," the case worker had explained.

I wondered who had made the complaint against Amil, but that didn't really matter. The most important thing was that there was a possibility that I would finally get custody. Fanci had also been very supportive about that. After putting the house that she shared with her husband up for sale she purchased a smaller home. Her mother was still in her home in Stone Mountain and so everything seemed to be working in her favor.

She still had the black BMW, so she convinced me to get my money back for the one that I had bought her. I kept it for myself instead. I kind of liked the Beemer, so I sold my Cadillac.

"I'm on my way over," Fanci had told me a few minutes earlier over the phone.

For some reason her voice didn't sound right. She'd been feeling bad the past couple days and we assumed that it was just stress. After the back and forth with the police she was cleared of any involvement in Isaac's death. Her alibi had checked out and witnesses had confirmed that she was where she'd said she was. I was just glad that it was all over with.

The sound of the doorbell urged me from my comfortable position on the sofa. I knew that it was Fanci because she would always ring the doorbell and then knock. When I opened the door she had a small plastic bag in her hand and there were tears in her eyes.

"You okay babe?" I asked before giving her a hug.

"Not really."

We separated so that I could let her inside. Once we were seated on the sofa I pulled her into my arms.

"What's wrong?" I rubbed her back soothingly and waited for her to tell me.

"I think I'm pregnant. I haven't seen my period this month."

A smile snuck up on my face, but she didn't seem to be happy about the possibility. "So, how late is it?"

"A few weeks. My period is like clockwork. It never…"

"I thought you wanted to have children baby. I mean a baby wouldn't be a bad thing, right?" I wanted her to be okay with it just in case, because I wasn't one for abortions and shit.

"I do, but I don't know if the timing is right."

"It's no such thing as right timing. A baby is a blessing either way. So, what's in the bag?"

"I bought two pregnancy tests and I wanted to take them here with you. I couldn't handle doing it by myself and Janai is at work...so..."

I nodded hoping they would both say that she was pregnant. She opened the bag and pulled the tests out.

"One is EBT and the other is Clear Blue Easy. I don't know which is better, so I just got them both."

"Okay, so what you waiting for ma. Go pee already." I smiled all hard at her and she managed to smile back.

"Alright." She sighed and walked down the hall to the restroom.

I was anxious as hell so I got up and stood outside of the door.

"You okay baby?" I asked.

"Yes," she called out. "I've done them both and I'm waiting."

"Uhhh, can I come in?"

"Sure."

I walked inside and pulled her into my arms. "We're gonna be good either way ma. We've been through some shit, but our love is real and strong, so we'll survive."

She nodded. "I know."

We kissed and then my eyes focused on the pregnancy tests that were on the counter. "Looks like we're having a little munchkin."

* * *

After making love all night in celebration of the new life that we had made, we were both sleeping hard as hell. When there was a loud knock at the door the next morning I just knew that it was Amil. Fanci didn't even wake up, and I didn't bother her. I would just get Amil's crazy ass to go away.

I looked out of the peephole and noticed two men standing there in suits. They had to be cops. Damn, what the fuck could they want? It was deja vu of what had happened at the hotel in Savannah. Without hesitation I opened the door and greeted them pleasantly.

They introduced themselves, pulled out their badges and then asked if they could come inside.

"You're not under arrest, but we need you to come to the station for questioning in the murder of

Isaac Moore," one of them stated with his lips in a straight line.

So they thought I had killed Fanci's husband.

"And may I ask a question?" I studied their faces as they obliged.

"Why am I being questioned for his murder? I don't know anything about it."

"We understand that you are in a relationship with his wife and you two had a fight not long before the murder occurred. We need to know about your whereabouts at the time of the murder. Yesterday we visited your business to retrieve surveillance video of the incident. The fight seemed really serious. We also have two witnesses who stated that you threatened to kill him," Detective Rodman said.

I did threaten to kill him, but I didn't mean it literally and I would never admit to it. There was nothing more that I could do other than complying and going to the station to answer their questions. First I had to call Gina and let her know that I wouldn't be coming to the shop anytime soon. That shit had my damn head hurting. Once they found out about my criminal past it was going to be all she wrote.

"I never threatened his life and I didn't kill him, but I will go to the station to answer any questions that you have. Can I make a phone call first and then go get my car keys."

Both of them nodded. I dialed Gina's number and she immediately started rambling. "The cops came with a search warrant. I tried to call you, but you didn't answer the damn phone. I think they think you killed that dude. Damn Devin, that bitch you fuckin' wit' done got you in some fucked up shit. That fight is makin' you look guilty as hell."

"I know. That's why I'm calling. I'm about to go the station so I won't be at the shop anytime soon. I'll call you back and keep you posted."

She let out a sharp breath. "Oh shit. Okay. I know that you didn't do anything. Nobody here said anything, but I'm sure he told somebody something before he died. That had to be why they came here all ready with a search warrant."

After we ended the call I went into my bedroom to get my car keys and to let Fanci know what was going on. I partially closed the door behind me, so that they wouldn't be suspicious, but I didn't want them to see her in my bed either.

"Fanci," I whispered as I gently shook her.

Her eyes fluttered open as she tried to focus on me. "Morning baby…"

"Shhhh…the cops are in there."

She suddenly shut up and mouthed, "Sorry."

"I have to go down to the station for questioning. They found out about the fight and got surveillance from my shop yesterday. They claim they got witnesses saying that I threatened to kill him. I'm going to need you to call my lawyer, because although I'm not under arrest yet, I think I will be. I'm going to drive my car, so if they arrest me call my boy Travis. I'll text you the number on my way out okay. He'll get my car and call my lawyer for me."

Tears welled up in her eyes as she nodded in agreement. "I love you," she whispered in my ear.

We kissed and then I reluctantly left her there to face the music. Karma was a motherfucker and it looked like that bitch had come to bite me in my ass.

* * *

"Right before his death he confided in his best friend about the fight and your threat to kill him. I know all about your criminal past and so making it look like a robbery must've been easy for you." Detective Rodman stared me down, but I didn't let him get to me.

"I didn't threaten to kill anybody and I didn't kill anybody. My past has nothing to do with this. I'm on parole and I haven't done anything to violate it. I would never risk going back to prison. All I do is work and take care of my daughter." I was not going to admit to doing something I didn't do. I didn't give a fuck how long they questioned me.

All I could think about was the fact that Fanci was pregnant and I was sitting there facing a murder charge. Then I thought about Londyn and what would happen to her if I did go to prison. If her mother was found unfit, who would she end up living with? The thought was really fucking with me.

"Were you having an affair with his wife?" Detective Newton asked with a smirk on his face. "She is a fine woman."

I wanted to punch him, but the fact that he was a cop stopped that urge. "He assumed that we were having an affair then, but I only did a tattoo for her. Over time, you know, after the fact, we have sparked up a relationship," I lied. If I admitted to it that would sound like I had a motive.

"Oh really?" Detective Rodman asked. "So, you mean to tell me that you wasn't sleeping with his wife and that man came to your place of business to fight you for no reason. Did you kill him so that you could have his wife? Was she in on it?"

"I'm telling you that I wasn't sleeping with his wife and some men are insecure. He thought it was an affair going on between us and there wasn't. I had no reason to kill him and I didn't kill him. I've been in fights before and I've never killed anybody. I was never charged or convicted of murder. No, I didn't kill him to have his wife and no she was not in on it with me, because I didn't do it." I had been there for an hour and my lawyer was on the way. In the meantime I knew what to say and what not to say.

"At first I thought your pretty little girlfriend had did it, but her alibi checked out. Where were you during the hours of ten pm and two am?" Detective Newton asked.

"I was home asleep." Damn, I knew that shit was weak, but it was true.

"Can anybody corroborate that?" Detective Rodman spat. "Because your girlfriend was obviously not with you."

I sighed. "No, but that's where I was. I watched a movie on Netflix and fell asleep. Look, have you all considered that it may have really been a robbery gone wrong and you're barking up the wrong tree."

"We have a search warrant to search your home that just went out. We'll find out if we are barking up the wrong tree or not. In the meantime you better lawyer up, because it's not looking good for you," that time Officer Newton was giving me the evil eye.

I just shook my head because I was feeling the tension. Damnit, suddenly my life had made a turn for the worst. What the fuck did I do to deserve that shit? I had nothing to do with that man's murder. Could they really arrest me because of all of that circumstantial shit? There were no witnesses who could put me at the scene of the crime. Could they charge me without a weapon?

Then I thought about the conversation I'd had with Fanci that night. Did she get somebody else to kill Isaac for her since I didn't agree to do it? Nah, she wouldn't do something like that. She wasn't capable, or was she? I had to get that thought out of my mind. There was no way that the woman I loved could plot a murder. That shit had to just be some crazy ass coincidence. If only I could've stopped that fight from happening. Then I wouldn't be in sitting there getting blamed for some bullshit that I didn't know anything about. It was fucked up how your past could make you look guilty even when you wasn't. Then I thought about the gun that was in my crib and the fact that they had probably already kicked my door down. Fuck!

By the time my lawyer got there almost two hours later I was already under arrest for a weapons charge. I was on parole as well as a felon, so I wasn't supposed to have a gun in my possession. If only I had thought about that shit I could've told Fanci to make sure that she got it out of there, but she didn't even know about it. The cops were slick. They got me out of the house first and then went to search my crib when I wasn't there. I wasn't prepared for that shit. Everything was falling apart and it was all because I had fallen in love with another man's wife. And despite that fact, I still loved her.

Epilogue

Fanci

Since they couldn't pin the murder on Devin for lack of evidence they got him for a gun charge instead. That was not only a parole violation, but it was also illegal because of his criminal past. All I did was cry when he called and told me that they had locked him up. At first he didn't have a bail, but then his lawyer finally got him a hearing. They finally granted him bail and he was out until his court trial.

I just enjoyed the short time that we had together and being pregnant did make it a little bit more joyous. For some reason, although I knew that Devin was facing time, the deep depression that I once felt was gone. Maybe it was because I was going to be a mother like I'd always wanted to be.

One emotion that I did feel though was guilt. I'd gotten everything I wanted, as far as finally having the chance to have a child and being financially stable. However, all of that seemed obsolete because I was facing losing my man for up to ten years. If it wasn't for my selfish, rash ass decision to conspire murder, my soulmate wouldn't be in the situation that he was in.

Although he didn't get the murder charge, they were still investigating him and trying to find more evidence to charge him. In the meantime they could hold him for something that had nothing to do with Isaac's death at all. Ballistics had proven that it wasn't the weapon that had killed him, but Devin was a victim of my circumstances. For that, I felt like shit.

At his sentencing I almost passed out because hearing them give him the maximum of ten years in prison made me weak. I was four months pregnant and seeing them take the love of my life away from me in handcuffs and shackles was too much for me to bear. I guess I was paying for my sins and I could only hope that I was at least a good mother.

Then I thought about my cousin Rod and the person who had killed Isaac with him. I couldn't tell on them even if I didn't care about incriminating myself. I would probably be killed before I made it to prison. Rod wouldn't be able to save me from the repercussions of the streets. I often thought about turning myself in, but I was afraid for my life. Therefore I had to deal with my guilt and try to have a healthy pregnancy despite everything else.

Iris, Lorraine and Megan still hated me, but they didn't bother me. I think they were all suspicious of me, but they knew that I had an alibi at the time of the murder. They didn't have anything on me, so they didn't have anything to say to me. I didn't care, because I didn't have to deal with them anymore. That was a relief.

As far as Amil, that bitch had left me alone completely. I guess she felt that I was reaping what I sowed and I was. She had managed to keep custody of Londyn and Devin told me that she'd moved to Alabama with some dude. He was distraught about it. All I could do was be there for him and face the fact that I would be giving birth to my child without him.

"I love you Fanci and I'm so sorry that things are the way they are," Devin said in a sweet voice over the phone.

I cherished our phone calls and was grateful that I could get him a cell phone in there.

"I love you too." If only he knew just how sorry I was. My hand drifted down to my belly and the thought of a baby boy or girl did make me feel some kind of solace. There was no way I could have my baby in prison and then give him or her up. I loved my mother, but I would not allow her to corrupt another child like she'd done me.

My punishment for what I had did was a life sentence of fear and being without the man that I loved for a decade, or more if they found a way to pin Isaac's murder on him. Something told me that I would continue to pay in some way, but I didn't know what was in store for me. All I knew was that although I loved Devin, I maybe should've thought twice about the decision to have an affair with him. That "D" had me fucked up though and because of it neither of our lives would ever be the same. It just further proved that what felt good was not always good for you.

The End

91753305R00146

Made in the USA
Middletown, DE
02 October 2018